# MICROSAURS
## FOLLOW THAT TINY-DACTYL

# MICROSAURS

## FOLLOW THAT TINY-DACTYL

## DUSTIN HANSEN

SQUARE FISH

Feiwel and Friends
New York

**SQUARE FISH**

An imprint of Macmillan Publishing Group, LLC
175 Fifth Avenue, New York, NY 10010
mackids.com

Square Fish and the Square Fish logo are trademarks of Macmillan and
are used by Feiwel and Friends under license from Macmillan.

Our books may be purchased in bulk for promotional, educational, or business use. Please
contact your local bookseller or the Macmillan Corporate and Premium Sales Department
at (800) 221-7945 ext. 5442 or by e-mail at MacmillanSpecialMarkets@macmillan.com.

Library of Congress Cataloging-in-Publication Data

Names: Hansen, Dustin, author, illustrator.
Title: Microsaurs: follow that tiny-dactyl / Dustin Hansen ; illustrated by Dustin Hansen.
Description: New York : Feiwel & Friends, 2017. | Series: Microsaurs ; 1 | Summary:
After spotting a miniature pterodactyl, Danny and his best friend Lin encounter
a mysterious invention that shrinks them down to the size of a raisin. Identifiers:
LCCN 2016027199 (print) | LCCN 2016047911 (ebook) | ISBN 9781250090218 (hardback) |
ISBN 9781250090225 (paperback) | ISBN 9781250090232 (Ebook) Subjects: | CYAC:
Pterodactyls—Fiction. | Dinosaurs—Fiction. | Size—Fiction. | Inventions—Fiction. |
Friendship—Fiction. | Adventure and adventurers—Fiction. | BISAC: JUVENILE FICTION /
Animals / Dinosaurs & Prehistoric Creatures. | JUVENILE FICTION / Social Issues / Friendship.
Classification: LCC PZ7.1.H3643 Fo 2017 (print) | LCC PZ7.1.H3643 (ebook) | DDC [Fic]—dc23
LC record available at https://lccn.loc.gov/2016027199

Originally published in the United States by Feiwel and Friends
First Square Fish edition, 2018
Book designed by Liz Dresner
Square Fish logo designed by Filomena Tuosto

10  9  8  7  6  5  4  3  2  1

LEXILE: 800L

*For my best adventuring partner, Jodi.*

*Who else?*

# CHAPTER 1

## ADVENTURE AWAITS

When your dad is the lead inventor for SpyZoom Technologies and your best friend is a skateboarding daredevil, there is no time to lead a boring life. And who'd want that anyway? The way I see it, adventure is all around us—we just have to go out and find it.

For example, just last year Lin and I helped my dad test out his new antigravity sleeping bag. Sure, we woke up on the roof of my neighbor's garage, but that was way more exciting than waking up in the same old bed every day for nine years.

And then there was the time Lin wanted to be a magician. She learned how to saw me in half without leaving a scratch, and she even learned how to make things disappear. Okay, we never found Lin's little sister's Wubby-Bunny, but still— it beat sitting around eating Cheezie-Poofs and watching *Electric Knight* reruns on TV.

But every year on July 18, our adventuring kicks up to a whole new level. That's when our hometown transforms from a quiet little place in the middle of nowhere to the loudest party on planet Earth.

Overnight the place fills up with skateboarders, news cameras, freestyle BMX riders, and fried-food trucks. Tourists show up to take selfies with the world-famous Ramp-O-Saurus, the tallest and greenest skate ramp in the western United States.

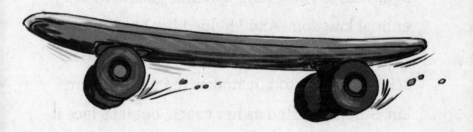

Fans don't just show up for the churros and corn dogs, although that is a pretty good reason. They come for the Under 12 X-treme Games. But this year was special, because the crowd favorite was my best friend, Lin Song.

It was Lin's second year competing in the U12X Games, but it was my first. Okay, so I wasn't actually competing. Ripping a 720 Heel Flip off a concrete half-pipe isn't really my thing. So I found better ways to get involved. For the past twelve months I helped Lin work on her nutrition, mostly by cutting down on gummy bears. I made her a practice schedule that included watching documentaries about flying squirrels, the best long-distance gliders in the animal kingdom. And I helped her beef up her chances with advanced technology and better science. Which totally makes me part of Team Lin. Sure, I'm listed as her coach, but let's face it, I'm way more than just a coach.

I'm Lin's secret weapon.

# CHAPTER 2
## AND THE CROWD GOES WILD!

I swiped the screen of my dad's hand-me-down smartphone, tapped on the SpyZoom app, and in less than a second I was staring right up Lin's nose. She was

futzing with the camera mounted on the top of her helmet. She noticed a little smudge on the lens, licked it, then wiped it clean with her shirtsleeve.

I tapped on the earpiece icon to activate the

SpyZoom Invisible Communicators, which were basically tiny earbud speakers you slipped into your ear that let you talk wirelessly without anyone noticing.

"So, Lin, how does that camera taste?" I said, and she giggled in my ear.

"Oh hi, Danny. I didn't know you were watching. I was making sure the camera was clean for the big jump," she said. "How does it look?"

"Spotless," I said. I tapped the GPS logo on the bottom left corner of the SpyZoom app, and the video feed of Lin swapped out for a map. A little red dot on the screen let me know that Lin was standing on top of the Ramp-O-Saurus and that she was moving exactly 0.01 miles per hour. "Hey, Lin, check to make sure the Micro-GPS Beacon is on tight one more time for me, would ya?"

"Sure thing," she said. I could hear her messing with her helmet as she made sure that my dad's latest invention, the SpyZoom Micro-GPS Beacon, was taped down on her helmet next to the camera. The video feed on my smartphone went all shaky and wobbly as she messed with her helmet, then she looked right back into the camera. "The beacon looks fine. I think we're ready."

"Sure, except I'm still looking up your nose,"
I said.

"Maybe you'll like this view better." Lin swung her helmet around, giving me a view of the crowd

from the top of the seventy-five-foot-tall Ramp-O-Saurus. And even though my feet were firmly on the ground, I still felt a little woozy as I watched the screen. The crowd cheered as one of Lin's competitors took his final run down the ramp.

"That was Ted Webster, everyone," the announcer said. "Looks like his jump of fifty-two feet, six inches won't be enough to send him to the finals this afternoon. But let's give him a hand before we send him on his way." His voice boomed out of the stack of speakers behind me. I felt every word rumble through my chest. For a split second I wished I could be on top of the Ramp-O-Saurus instead of Lin. But then I remembered that nobody in this entire crowd showed up to watch me get sick on top of a seventy-five-foot-tall skate ramp. Heights and I are not the best of friends.

I looked back at the video. Lin was strapping on her helmet again, and the dizzy way-too-high-in-the-air feeling returned. She looked down at the crowd and I waved. I could see myself on the screen, and I looked like an ant in a red T-shirt.

"You know, I think you may be a little bit crazy," I said to Lin.

"I am crazy, Danny, but it's my own brand of crazy. I'm totally used to it," Lin said.

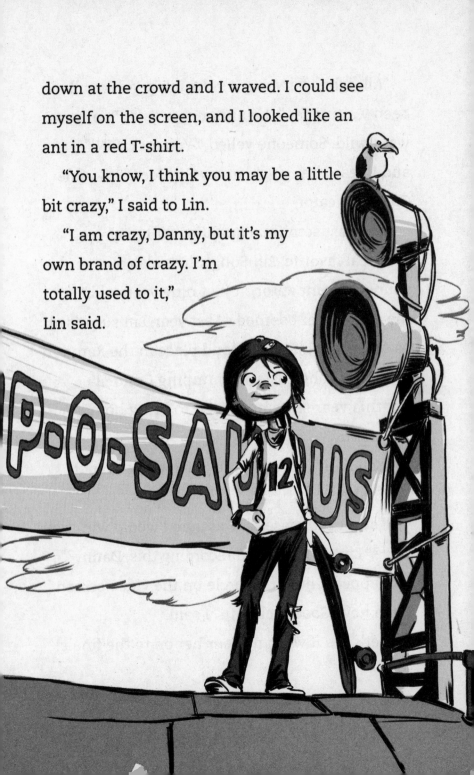

"All right, everyone, it's the jump you've all been waiting for," the announcer said. The crowd went wild. Someone yelled, "You rock, LIN!" and I heard her giggle in my SpyZoom Invisible Communicator.

"Our last semifinal qualifier for today is a local favorite, Lin Song. She's also our youngest competitor, at just nine years old," the announcer boomed. "Last year, Lin surprised us all by finishing in second place in the Ramp-O-Saurus Long Distance Jumping Contest. But this year she's promised to bring home the trophy."

"You didn't surprise me one bit last year," I said to Lin.

"I surprised myself. I was sure I would win first place," Lin said. "Are you recording this, Danny?"

I tapped a little red circle on the video screen. "I am now. Good luck, Lin!" I said.

"Let's see if we can cheer her on to the finals!

3, 2, 1 . . . GO!" the announcer shouted, and the
crowd went totally nutso! I was screaming, too,
but when you're only nine years old, even if
you are tall for your age, it's hard to see over a
hollering horde. But that didn't matter, because
I had the best view in the crowd. I looked at the
screen as Lin launched herself down the ramp.

Watching Lin zip down the back of the Ramp-
O-Saurus made my teeth chatter and my hands
sweaty. I had to stop myself from running and
jumping and throwing fake karate punches just
to let off a little of my energy.

The GPS tracker was going crazy, beeping and
blinking to tell me Lin had broken her previous
speed record: 27.2 miles per hour and going
faster every second. She crouched over and
tucked down. I crouched, too. I couldn't help
it. Then, just as she reached the bottom of the
ramp, something reddish-orange *whacked* into
the camera lens.

I yelped and shot straight up in the air. Good thing I was in a crowd of screaming, jumping fans, because I fit right in.

The reddish-orange splat was only on the screen for a split second, then it flew away and all I could see was sky. Then ground, then sky, then ground, then sky—then finally the big pit filled with foam chunks. The crowd roared as Lin finished her qualifying jump.

"WOW, did you see that, skate fans? Lin Song pulled off a perfect Triple Back Flip before she landed in the pit," the announcer shouted.

Lin's voice exploded in my ear. It was so loud that the SpyZoom Invisible Communicator nearly popped right out. "That was . . . AMAZING!"

"And it's official, folks. Lin Song's distance is fifty-eight feet, four inches! Which not only qualifies her for this afternoon's championship Ramp-O-Saurus event, but it puts her in second place, right behind last year's winner, B.J. Hooper!"

"You did it! Did you hear that, Lin?" I asked. I tried to make my way to the foam pit, but the crowd was crazy, chanting Lin's name over and over again. I knew she was talking into my SpyZoom Invisible Communicator, but I couldn't hear a word she was saying over the wild crowd. I checked the video feed as a bunch of fans nearly smothered Lin as she climbed from the pit. They rushed her and asked for her autograph. It was pretty much the coolest thing I've ever seen, and I could only imagine how crazy it would be later now that she had qualified for the finals.

I pulled out the checklist I'd prepared for today's qualifying jump. Only two things remained on the list to cross off before I could call it a complete success.

✔ Check GPS

✔ Check SpyZoom Invisible Communicators

✔ Check video feed

✔ Watch Lin jump to victory

Buy celebration Corn dogs!

Meet by the bike rack

"I'm going to get the celebration corn dogs. See you by the bikes after you break away from your fans. You rocked that Ramp-O-Saurus!"

Lin said something like "extra mustard," and I knew that she heard the message. As I walked to the corn-dog stand, there was one thing I couldn't get off my mind. It was the strange reddish-orange thing that smacked into the camera. I had to know what it was, and I couldn't wait to check the video and do a little research.

# CHAPTER 3
## FOLLOW THAT SMUDGE

The grass next to the bike racks was cool as I sat down and watched the video of Lin's jump again.

I was munching my corn dog when I noticed something strange on the SpyZoom app. The GPS tracker was telling me that Lin wasn't in the park at all. In fact, according to the app, it looked

like she was still zooming along at nearly fifteen miles per hour, right out of the skate park and heading toward the center of town.

I checked the video feed, but that didn't help. It only made things more confusing. Lin was still standing in the middle of a crowd of fans, using a bright blue marker to autograph everything from skateboards to sandwich wrappers. There was something strange going on. I turned the SpyZoom app off, then launched it again, but it was still acting wacko.

"Hey, Lin, your corn dog is getting cold," I said. "And somehow my SpyZoom app thinks you're in two places at once."

"Unless your dad glued a cloning device into my helmet, I'd say that's impossible," she said into the Invisible Communicator. I heard her tell people that was all the autographs for now, using the world's best excuse: cold corn dogs are gross.

I smiled to myself because she didn't know how close to the truth she was. My dad *was* working on a top secret cloning device in his home laboratory that very day. But it wasn't the cloning device that caused the problem. It was something else, I just knew it. My first thought was that when the reddish-orange thing hit the camera on Lin's helmet, it must have knocked off the GPS beacon, and Lin's jump had so much force that the seed-sized tracking device had been launched down Main Street.

I decided to watch the video and look for clues. I played back Lin's jump and scrolled to the point where the *whack* happened.

I found the blurry reddish-orange blob, all smooshed up against the screen, and I tapped the screen to pause the video.

"Whatcha doing, Danny? Checking out the second-longest jump in Ramp-O-Saurus history?" Lin said, only this time it wasn't in the

SpyZoom Invisible Communicator—she was standing right in front of me.

"You got over here fast," I said as I tweaked the video playback screen.

"What can I say? The threat of cold corn dogs moves me,"

she said with her hand held out. I tossed her the corn dog and she sat in the grass next to me. "Thanks, but really. Are you checking out my jump?"

"Kind of," I said. "Oh yeah, forgot this." I pulled six packets of bright yellow mustard out of my pocket and gave them to her.

"Thanks again. Getting the second-longest Ramp-O-Saurus jump ever really wears a girl out. Did I mention it was the SECOND-LONGEST JUMP IN RAMP-O-SAURUS HISTORY OF FOREVER?" she said as she squished three packets of mustard on her corn dog.

"Once or twice, yeah." I was moving through the video one frame at a time, trying to find a better look at the thing that smacked her helmet. "Something hit you just before you jumped."

"Really? I didn't feel anything," Lin said through a mouthful of yellow goop.

"Yeah, look at this." I showed her the image.

"Looks like a smudge of ketchup. Ketchup is gross," she said as she opened her fourth pack of mustard.

"Ha. It does look like a ketchup smudge." I forwarded the video a couple of frames and the blob started to take shape. The blurry edges turned into batlike wings and a long, alligator-like snout. It was the strangest creature I've ever seen, and I started to wonder if maybe there was something wrong with the camera. Maybe the whole SpyZoom app was on the fritz.

Then I tapped the video forward one more frame and for a moment I was so shocked that I forgot to breathe.

"Earth to Danny." Lin nudged my shoulder. "Are you okay?"

I blinked. "Um, Lin, I need to show you something, but you're not going to believe it."

I turned the
screen so
she could
get a better
look.

"Wow,
yeah,
that's
one big
cricket,"
she said,
her teeth the
color of the sun.

"That's not a
cricket," I said. A funny
feeling flew through my stomach. It was telling
me I was either onto the greatest discovery in
the history of histories, or I was going crazy-
wacko-loony-nutso. Either way, it was pretty
exciting and I had to tell Lin. "I think it's a

dinosaur. And not only that, I think it has the GPS beacon in its mouth and is flying out of town with it."

"I hate to break this to you, Danny. I know you're all sciencey and I'm not, but there are two things you might have overlooked. First, the dinosaurs died, like, five hundred bazillion years ago or something," she said.

"Actually, it was only sixty-five million years ago," I corrected.

"Details," she said, then wiped her mouth on her arm, leaving behind a yellow mustard smear. "But the second thing is the biggie, and I know you know what I'm going to say here. The dinosaurs were HUGE-MONGOUS! Bigger than elephants. Bigger than whales. Bigger than the Ramp-O-Saurus!" she said, and her eyes went all wide and round when she said Ramp-O-Saurus, because to Lin the green skate ramp was the biggest thing in her life.

I have at least fifteen books on dinosaurs at home, so I'm pretty much an expert on the whole dinosaur subject. I could have given Lin a list of about fifty dinosaurs that were actually smaller than a birthday cake, but she did have a point.

"True. Most dinosaurs *were* huge, but my dad says that science never sleeps. What if they changed somehow? What if the dinosaurs evolved into something small? Something so small that they could be mistaken for a ketchup-colored cricket, for example?" I stood up, because I had to get my dad's GPS beacon back and I wanted—no, I NEEDED—to see the critter that stole the beacon with my own eyes.

"Let me see it again," Lin said. I handed her my smartphone before I slipped my back-pack on.

Lin studied the image while I tightened my shoelaces. She rotated it and looked at it upside down. She narrowed her eyes and rubbed her chin in a way that meant she was really thinking hard. Then, a surprised grin slowly spread across her face.

"So? What do you think?"

"I have to be back in three hours so I can beat B.J. Hooper on the Ramp-O-Saurus. You know that, right?"

"Oh yeah, I know. So, what are you saying?"

"What I'm saying is, let's go catch a dinosaur," Lin replied.

# CHAPTER 4
# ENTER AT YOUR OWN RISK

L in and I had cruised up and down Main Street hundreds of times—wait, make that thousands of times—in the past. But today there was no cruising. Today, we RAN, because when you're chasing a ketchup-colored, prehistoric, flying bat-lizard-gator thing, cruising just will not do.

Stopping every block to check the GPS tracker

slowed us down a bit, but still it didn't take long for us to catch up to the flying beacon thief.

The little guy led us just outside of town, to an old dirt path that we would have totally missed if we weren't using my dad's SpyZoom technology. Gigantic trees lined both sides of the shady path. They were so old their long, twisted branches reached down to touch the ground.

"I've never seen this place before. It's giving me the creeps," Lin said, and I was glad she said it first, because that's exactly how I was feeling.

"Yeah. It's spooky," I agreed.

Lin slipped around me and started right down the tree-lined path.

"What are you doing?" I asked.

Lin stopped and turned to look back at me. "I like spooky," she said, like it was the most normal thing in the world. "Are you coming?"

All of a sudden my throat felt dry and my legs were wobbly. Before I could answer I unclipped

my 0.75-liter, Official Issue, U.S. Army canteen from my belt. "Um, sure, yeah. Of course I'm coming. I just need to hydrate first." I took a swig of lukewarm water, then passed the canteen to Lin. "I like spooky, too," I said. But I'm not sure I was telling the truth.

Lin and I ran side by side down the twisty path until we were both out of breath.

"Are we," she panted, "still going in the . . . right direction?"

I checked the GPS tracker. "Yeah, we're so close we could see it any second now," I said.

We tiptoed around another bend in the path and right there in the middle of nowhere was a big iron fence. The space between the bars was so wide you could just about ride a bike through them, but a fence like this meant one thing and one thing only. Stay OUT!

"Dang," Lin said. "That's the oldest house I've ever seen."

The dark brick house stretched up above the trees. It was a cross between a haunted mansion and a friendly old grandpa's house. Pterodactyl-shaped gargoyles snarled down from the corners of the pointed roof, and a statue of a velociraptor on the lawn made the house look even more dangerous. But the front door was painted the happiest shade of pink I'd ever seen, and there was a bright yellow porch swing with cushions so fluffy and white they reminded me of homemade marshmallows.

"And I thought the tree-lined path was spooky," I said.

Lin tossed her skateboard through the iron bars, then squeezed in so fast I didn't have time to stop her.

"What are you doing now?" I asked.

"I told you. I like spooky," Lin said. Her entire face was grinning; even her nostrils and eyebrows and the tips of her hair looked happy.

"Come on, Danny. You know you can't let me go adventuring by myself."

I was about to suggest we go adventuring in a place without a velociraptor statue and an iron gate when I heard a little *Eeep!* I looked up and froze. There it was, the ketchup-colored GPS beacon thief. It was perched on the tip of the statue's nose. I tilted my head and raised my shoulders at it, kind of asking what I should do, and I swear I saw the little critter wink right at me just before it flew away behind the house.

Lin was right. Even if I was feeling all jitter-buggy in my stomach, there was no way I was going to miss out on this adventure. I dried my sweaty hands on my pants, then slipped my backpack off and pushed it through the iron bars.

"I wouldn't miss this for a year's supply of Big Moe's double bacon cheeseburgers," I said, and then I grinned because it was true. I'd take adventure over double bacon cheeseburgers any day. Especially an adventure with a real-life dinosaur involved.

Behind the iron fence, Lin and I found ourselves standing in grass up to our knees.

"Do you think anyone lives here?" I whispered as I checked the GPS tracker.

"Hello! Is there anybody here?" Lin shouted, and I cringed. Stealth wasn't her thing.

"Looks abandoned to me," I said.

The little critter was really close now, so I stopped Lin and we scanned the area for it. I was about to give up when I heard the *Eeep!* noise again.

"There. On the tree branch," I said as I pointed to the little orange creature. I know it sounds strange, but I had a feeling that it was waiting for us. Like it wanted to be found.

"What is it?" Lin whispered. "It's really cute."

"I think it's a pterodactyl," I said.

"A terra-what-el?" Lin asked.

"A pterodactyl. A flying dinosaur from the Jurassic period," I explained.

"Hey, little Jurassic buddy. Come here." Lin

whistled as she inched forward. She held out her hand and wiggled her fingers like she was petting an imaginary dog. "We won't hurt you."

The tiny pterodactyl tilted its head and looked at us like *we* were the strange creatures that arrived from sixty-five million years ago, then it *eeep*ed again, flapped its batlike wings, and zoomed out of sight as fast as buttered lightning.

We didn't need to discuss it—we both chased after it at a full run!

The backyard was even more overgrown than the front. Patches of dry weeds stretched up to my belt loops, and an empty doghouse sat in the shadow of an old barn, twice as run-down as the spooky mansion.

"The ptera-whoozle-whatcha-call-it went in through that crack in the door," Lin said, pointing to a wide barn door that was about to fall right to the ground. Next to the door there was a rusted metal sign nailed to a post about a foot taller than me. Painted on the sign in big purple letters were the words:

IF YOU ARE LESS THAN 65 MILLION YEARS OLD Enter at Your OWN RISK!

"Whoever lived here knew something about dinosaurs that we don't know," I said.

"Why do you say that?" Lin asked.

"If you're less than sixty-five million years old? Well, that's just about everyone, except . . ." I started to explain before Lin finished my sentence.

"Our flying Jurassic buddy."

"Exactly," I said.

I pulled my smartphone out of my backpack and started videoing the place. I got a good shot of the old barn, and I was scanning the hand-painted sign, when I heard a big *creeeeak!* I panned the camera over just in time to see Lin sneaking in through the big barn door.

I couldn't believe she was barging in. "What are you doing now?" I asked while the camera was still recording.

"I'm entering at my own risk," she said,
completely ignoring the sign. Then she
disappeared into the dark, shadowy barn.

# CHAPTER 5
# THE SECRET BARN-LAB-LIBRARY THINGY

The inside of the old, run-down barn was totally different from the outside. It didn't look abandoned at all. There were a couple of lamps left on, and it smelled like someone had just gobbled down a bag of microwaved popcorn a few minutes earlier. Not to mention the outside of the barn was huge, but the inside was no bigger than my bedroom back home.

"This place is so cool," I said as I followed Lin into the barn. We were standing in a small room that couldn't make up its mind if it was a forgotten library, a science lab, or a secret hideout.

"I want to touch everything in this entire place," Lin said as she started exploring with her eyes and fingers.

I checked the GPS tracker. It looked like the tiny dinosaur was behind the wall at the back of the room, which didn't make sense. There wasn't even a door there.

Being in the barn-lab-library-hideout was exciting, but I couldn't shake the feeling that we were being watched, or that any second now someone would catch us snooping and throw us in jail. Or worse, summer school!

"Have you seen one of these before?" Lin said. She was studying a fish tank tucked into a bookshelf. I stopped digging through a box of old rocks and joined her.

An odd creature that looked half swimming snail and half miniature squid swam around inside a glowing fish tank. "Nope, but it reminds me of a fossil I saw in a book once. And there are dinosaur bones all over the place, too." I pointed around the room at the fossils on the shelves, stuffed in between glass specimen jars and books so big you'd need a forklift to carry them home. "It looks like the person who lived here was a scientist. A paleontologist, or something like that."

"What's a paleontologist?" Lin asked.

"A scientist who studies dinosaurs," I explained as I looked around. There were microscopes and magnifying glasses on a cluttered workbench. I peeked through a large magnifying glass to get a closer look at what I thought was a small pile of dust. But under the magnifying glass the dust turned out to be a nest and three speckled eggshells.

"Do you think I should feed it?" Lin asked

from across the room. I turned around just in time to see her sprinkling a handful of dry Fruity Stars cereal into the top of the odd fish tank.

"Too late now, I guess," I said.

"It likes it," Lin said, and she clapped her hands. "Who knew that swimming snail-squids liked Fruity Stars?"

"You're probably the first person to discover that in the history of the world." I rolled my eyes. "Come check this out." I pointed to the magnifying glass with the little nest, then I slid over for her to look at it while I moved over to check out one of the microscopes.

"Are those eggs?"

I looked into the microscope, found the focus knob, and twisted while I answered. "They were eggs. Now they're eggshells. They've already hatched."

"Do you think they could be mini-pterodactyl eggs?" Lin asked.

My heart did a flip-flop. "You might be right!" I said, but even thinking about what that meant made me dizzy. I still wasn't 100 percent sure that the GPS beacon thief was a dinosaur, and now we were looking at a nest with three eggshells—which could mean only one thing. More tiny pterodactyls.

"Hey, do you think we traveled back in time?" Lin asked as she picked up a jar filled with leaves soaking in some kind of blue jelly.

"My dad says time travel is impossible. But I just found another clue." I leaned back and offered the microscope to Lin. I couldn't help but smile because I knew she was going to go nutso when she saw what was inside the microscope.

Lin looked into the eyepiece. "It's a note."

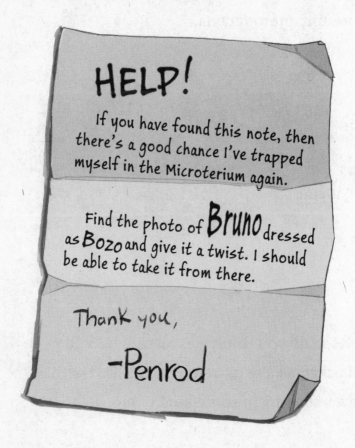

# HELP!

If you have found this note, then there's a good chance I've trapped myself in the Microterium again.

Find the photo of **Bruno** dressed as Bozo and give it a twist. I should be able to take it from there.

Thank you,

-Penrod

Lin looked up at me. "What's a Penrod?"

"I'll bet Penrod is a who, not a what. I'm wondering what a Bruno is, though," I said as I looked around the cluttered lab.

"Bruno is a dog!" Lin said as she held up a framed photo of a wrinkly bulldog wearing a black helmet and a black cape. She started laughing.

"What's so funny?" I asked.

"There's a green sticker on the frame that says 'Bruno as Arf Vader' on it. Get it? Arf Vader?" She showed me the picture again and I totally got the joke.

"Let's find the Bruno as Bozo picture."

We looked around and found more framed photos of Bruno dressed as famous people like Bilbo Waggins, Sherlock

SHERLOCK BONES

Bones, Winnie the Poodle, and my favorite, Bruno as Hairy Pawter.

But no matter how hard we looked, we couldn't find Bruno as Bozo.

"All right. We know Bruno is a dog, but who's Bozo?" I asked.

"I think he was a clown. Bozo the Clown, ya know?" she said, and something sparked in my mind.

"Of course! I've seen it five times already. It's right here." I pointed to a framed picture of Bruno the slobbery bulldog wearing a bright rainbow-colored

wig and a fake red
nose. "It was hanging
on the wall all along."

"Well, what are you
waiting for? Give it a
twist and let's go save
this Penrod guy," Lin
said.

I reached up and
took the picture in both hands, but it wouldn't
come off the wall. I gave the picture a twist
and a clicking sound
*tink-tink-tink*ed behind
the wooden wall at the
back of the small room.
Everything started to
rumble and shake; even
a bit of the water from
the fish tank sloshed to
the floor.

"What's going on?" Lin asked.

"I don't know. Maybe we better—" I started.

Running, screaming, even hiding under the desk were all things that crossed my mind, but they were all drowned out by my curiosity as the back wall of the secret barn-lab-library room began to lower.

A cloud of steam poured over the wall and filled the dry air of the small barn-lab-library-hideout, as a jungle was revealed behind the secret wall. I couldn't believe what I was looking at: a real-life, honest-to-goodness, vines-hanging-from-bright-green-trees, ferns-and-mushrooms-on-the-soggy-soil jungle.

"Holy pepperoni pizza," I said.

"With extra cheese," Lin added for gooeyness' sake.

The wall thumped as it lowered all the way down, and Lin and I tiptoed forward.

"Mr. Penrod. Are you in here?" I asked, but nobody answered.

"Maybe he's asleep," Lin suggested.

There was a metal step just inside the fresh-smelling jungle, and I stood on it to get a better look. Below the step it looked like someone had spilled a desk drawer of office supplies: staplers, pushpins, sticky notes, and stamp pads. A red-and-white drinking straw reached up from a pile of rubber bands and leaned against the metal step. I noticed someone had taped the straw to the side of the step. I was trying to imagine why someone would tape a straw to anything when Lin walked out onto the step with me. With the two of us on it, the step dropped an inch, and something clicked into place. A sound that reminded me of a cross between a video game spaceship and a vacuum cleaner whirled above our heads. I looked up just in time to see a bright blue light flash on. It all happened so fast that I didn't even have time to think about moving out of the way.

The blue light felt cool and sparkly. It was like being stuffed in a freezer full of glitter for a second, and then the cold feeling was gone.

"Uh, Danny. I think the barn is growing. A lot."

"Either that, or we're . . ."

"SHRINKING!" we both yelled as we realized what was going on.

In less than a second, I'd gone from being the fourth-tallest kid at Jefferson Elementary to the second-smallest kid on Earth. I couldn't get my thoughts right. Nothing made sense. The tiny dinosaur, the living fossil in the fish tank, and now Lin and I were the size of a couple of raisins. And not plump, juicy raisins, either. More like dried-up raisins that had been dropped under the couch and forgotten about for a year and three months.

Lin started running around on the metal step, which was about three times bigger than a soccer field. She was waving her hands above her head, flailing around and shouting like a crazy person. "I'm the size of a bug! Help me! I've been shrinkified and I AM THE SIZE OF A BUG!"

I tried not to get caught up in her crazy, but it is next to impossible not to freak out when you realize that you are suddenly very squashable. I ran around for a while, too, waving my arms and

shouting for help, then somehow I ran out of breath and found the whole situation hilarious at the same time.

I started laughing so hard that I couldn't run around and freak out anymore, which made Lin pause. She looked at me and started laughing, too. I fell to my knees, holding my sides because they were starting to ache, then I rolled onto my back and looked up toward the sky as I tried to catch my breath.

The barn that we once stood in was so large that it faded away in the misty air around us. The metal step was cool against my back and I took a few deep breaths and started to think again because I had a feeling if we wanted to unshrink again someday, thinking was going to be important.

"What just happened, Danny?" Lin asked. "Is this even possible?"

"If you would have asked me that thirty

seconds ago, I would have said no." I pointed to the drinking straw taped to the metal stair. "But that red-and-white straw is bigger than the Ramp-O-Saurus, so I'd have to say it's more than possible. I think it actually happened. The real question is, what do we do now?" I asked.

# CHAPTER 6
## THE MICROTERIUM

L in zipped down the straw like a pro, landing with a perfect dismount. I, however, tumbled all the way down, rolling head over heels, until the straw spit me out at the bottom in a big poof of dust, but that didn't mean I didn't enjoy it.

"That was awesome!" I said. "If I could get back up there, I'd do it again."

"Let's try," Lin said as she started kicking around the office supplies from the spilled drawer, looking for something to help her climb back up the step.

I stood up and dusted off my shorts. We were standing in the shadow of the step, and I looked up. It was at least ten times taller than me. AT LEAST! I wasn't so sure I'd want to climb up there even if Lin found a way. "I think we better try to find this Penrod guy first. Maybe he knows a way to unshrink us."

"Is unshrink even a word?" Lin asked. She found a paper clip bigger than a surfboard and she was tying a piece of dental floss that looked like a big waxy rope to it.

"I don't know if unshrink is a word, but it's what we need to do," I said.

"So, this is Microland, eh?"

"Penrod called it the Microterium in the note. But no matter what you call it, it's pretty strange."

"Ya think?" Lin said. She pulled on the dental-floss rope, lifting one end of the paper clip up as high as her knee, then letting it fall to the ground. It kicked up a little cloud of dust. "Boom!"

I guess in a way I should have been scared, or worried, but it was just the

opposite. My mind buzzed with new ideas and thoughts about being small enough to ride an ant. I had a lot of questions about the place, but first I wanted to know if my technology worked after it had been zapped so small. The first thing I checked was the video camera on my smartphone, and it worked perfectly.

I guess when you're regular size you really miss the details, because now that I was the size of a garden pea, everything looked brand-new to me. The whole place was green and alive. What I thought was moss before was actually fields of leafy plants and knee-high grass. What would have looked like an ordinary rock to me a few minutes ago now looked like a boulder so big it would crush a house.

But that wasn't the half of it. The place was covered in plants I'd never seen before. Orange flowers with blossoms the size of a large pizza, long spiky plants with leaves that looked like a pirate's sword, and mushrooms so big you could take a nap under one and never worry about getting a sunburn. I was videoing a group of plants that reminded me of a row of bright blue trumpets when I heard a snort.

"Nice one, Danny," Lin said with a little laugh.

"Um, that wasn't me," I said. I turned to look back at Lin. She'd been playing with a stamp pad and her hands were dark blue.

Just then, something HUGE rumbled in the grass behind Lin. It made a half-barking, half-snorting sound and I forgot every word in the dictionary except one.

"RUN!"

A creature nearly the size of a minivan burst through the tall grass behind Lin. It had three horns, big feet, and a crest of leather and bone behind its head.

"That way!" Lin shouted, pointing to a line of rock cliffs just on the other side of a little creek lined with purple mushrooms.

Part of me was terrified, but an even bigger part of me was thinking this was the best day EVER! I mean, I was being chased by a real, live dinosaur!

Luckily, the terrified part controlled my legs, so I turned and ran as fast I could.

I shouted ahead to Lin. "We're being chased by a triceratops!"

"I KNOW!" Lin shouted back. She laughed as she ran, and I could tell that a part of her was loving this as much as I was.

Being chased by a three-horned dinosaur made Lin run even faster than normal, and before long she'd left me in the dust. Lin parkoured over the mushrooms and sprinted through the little creek so fast I wondered if her shoes even got wet. She bounced up the other side of the creek and slipped into a crack in the rock wall in a flash.

My backpack bounced on my back, making it hard to really get moving, and by the time I made it to the mushrooms I could feel the hot breath of the dinosaur behind me. I launched over the mushrooms and splashed down in the creek and realized that the excited part of me had gone. All that was left was the terrified part.

Turns out having a triceratops chase you through a jungle was not as fun as I had imagined. The dino splashed behind me, and for the first time in as long as I could remember, I wished I'd left my backpack home. At the very least I should have left behind the pineapple I planned on eating for lunch. Canned pineapple is extra heavy when you're running away from a two-thousand-pound triceratops.

My legs burned as I sloshed out of the creek and glopped my feet down on the muddy bank. I took one big step out of the mud when the nose of the triceratops bumped into my backpack, sending me facedown in the mud.

I landed so hard that everything went black for a second. I could smell the dinosaur's breath all around me. It smelled like old broccoli and dirty gym socks. I was too afraid to open my eyes, but I remembered something my dad told me. He said, above all things, a scientist is brave.

I rolled over on my back and braved a little peek. The sharp, bone-like beak of a triceratops was less than an inch from my nose.

# CHAPTER 7
# THE GRASS CLUMP MAN

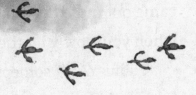

The massive beast sniffed, creating a vacuum with its nostrils that snuffled a handful of hair right up its nose. It blinked a few times, sniffed again, and wrinkled its big wrinkly nose, then sneezed right in my face.

The dino half smiled at me, as if this was fun for the both of us, then stuck out its big pink tongue and licked my red shirt and grumbled deep in its chest.

Covered in dino sneeze, mud, and slobber, I closed my eyes again because I was too afraid to see what would come next. I figured I was about to be smooshed, or snacked on, and I let out a little noise that was supposed to be "help" but it came out more like that squeaky noise you hear when you slowly let the air out of a balloon.

"Hiiiiii-YAH!" someone shouted. It sounded like an old bear who'd just earned a black belt in karate.

"Heeeey-you-Two-EEE!" he shouted again, and both the dinosaur and I looked in the direction of the shouting man. All I could see was a man-shaped clump of ferns and grass, but then it moved and I saw the reflection off the grass clump's glasses.

I didn't know what was scarier, the triceratops standing over me, or the wild man shouting

nonsense words with twigs and grass twisted
into his hair and mustache. The Grass Clump
Man carried a large stick. He
waved it around his head, which
was covered in spiky red grass.
I didn't think it was possible

for the day to get any stranger, but I was wrong.

"Over here, you big overgrown puppy!" Grass Clump Man shouted as he smashed the stick down on the ground. It snapped into three pieces. He picked up the shortest piece, then from somewhere deep inside his grassy suit, he pulled out a large jar of peanut butter. He dipped one hand in the peanut butter, then smeared it all over the stick before he threw it across the creek.

"Go get it, Twoee!" Grass Clump Man shouted.

The triceratops that had me pinned to the ground splashed through the creek, chasing after the stick. Its tongue drooped from its mouth like a big goofy puppy.

Grass Clump Man ran my way, moving just as slow as you'd expect a man covered in ferns and grass to run. The muddy ground didn't want to let me up, but I slurped out of the brown goop and scrambled to my feet. Lin came flying off the bank and landed between me and Grass Clump Man. She was swinging her skateboard over her head like a pirate sword, and she wore a snarl on her face.

"Stop right there!" Lin shouted, and Grass Clump Man obeyed. I knew Lin was brave, but I'd never seen this side of her. I knew Lin wasn't the type to actually clobber someone with a skateboard, but I could tell by the look in his eyes that Grass Clump Man wasn't taking any chances.

"Hang on, hang on. I'm only trying to help," Grass Clump Man said. The closer he got, the less crazy he looked, and I let out a breath I didn't even know I was holding.

"We need to hurry, before Twoee finishes his snack. Something about your arrival has changed his behavior. It's fascinating, but when you're Twoee's size, fascinating can become dangerous in an instant." While he said this, the Grass Clump Man smothered one of the stick pieces in more peanut butter.

The man whistled, and the triceratops stopped chomping on his treat and looked our way. His head poked up over the tall reeds on the bank.

The big beastie tilted his head, lolled out his tongue, and barked. I tried to feel scared or maybe even worried, but he reminded me so much of a big puppy that I kind of just wanted to run across the creek and scratch his belly.

The Grass Clump Man threw the next stick and the big dino bounced after it.

"All right. That will buy us a few minutes." He licked the peanut butter off his fingers, then stuffed the jar of peanut butter into a secret pocket inside his grass-covered suit. "Are you ready?"

"Um, ready for what?" Lin asked.

"To head back to my lab," the Grass Clump Man said. "We need to get out of here before Twoee finishes his snack. It will give us more time to figure out what is making him act so strange."

"You mean acting like a dog? That seems pretty strange to me," I said.

"No, no, no. That's totally normal behavior for Twoee. It's why I named him after my dog,

Bruno. His real name is Bruno 2, but I call him Twoee for short." The Grass Clump Man looked so proud to have named the triceratops after his dog, and it clicked in my mind.

"You're Penrod. Lin and I saw your note in the microscope and came to save you," I said.

"Professor Penbrook Penrod, actually. Glad you found my note. I hope you brought the juice," he said. Twoee chuffed and barked from across the creek.

I shrugged my shoulders and looked at Lin. "We didn't know that we were supposed to bring juice. Danny has a water bottle," she said.

"It's a canteen, actually. Official Army Issue," I explained.

"Well, we'll top that taco with cheese when the time comes." He threw the last stick chunk to Twoee. "Right now, we need to go." He turned and stomped his big grass-covered feet through a tall crop of weeds, and in a second he was gone.

"You know he's completely insane, right?" Lin said.

"Do we follow him?" I asked Lin, and she rolled her eyes at me like I was asking the most obvious question in the universe.

"Wait for us, Professor," Lin shouted, then we chased after our new jungle guide.

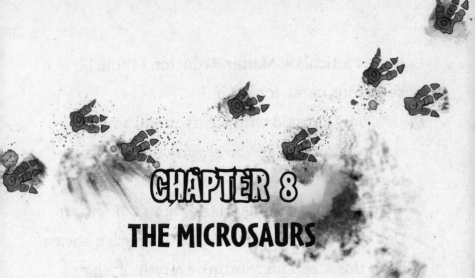

# CHAPTER 8
# THE MICROSAURS

It wasn't hard catching up to the grass-covered professor, but by the time we had, my mind was full of questions.

"Did you invent the shrink-a-fier thingy?" Lin asked.

"Huh. Shrink-A-Fier, I like that," Professor Penrod said. "I did invent it, but I've been calling it the Particulate Matter Reductor. I think I'll keep your name for it, Lin."

"Cool," Lin said with a very proud smile.

"So, I don't get it. You shrunk the dinosaurs too?" I asked.

"Oh no, not at all. And they aren't dinosaurs, Danny. They are MICROSAURS. They have always been this size. I just shrunk everything else to fit their world." He looked at me and winked. "Myself included."

"Where did you find the Microsaurs?" Lin asked. She crouched under a fallen log, and I climbed over it.

"Well, it all goes back to this notebook." Professor Penrod reached inside his grass suit and pulled out a leather-bound book about the size of my dad's wallet. "It was sent to me from my favorite uncle, a paleontologist and professor with a fantastic name."

"Let me guess, his name was Professor
Penrod, too," Lin said.

"Precisely, Lin. Very smart." He handed me
the leather-bound notebook and I checked it out

as we made our way to his lab. "I hadn't seen my uncle Penrod in more than twenty years. In fact, nobody had. He'd just disappeared. Last we heard from him, he'd been studying fossils in a jungle in Peru. Imagine my surprise when I received this notebook in the mail."

"Wow, this is so cool," I said as I turned the pages in the book. It was filled with drawings of the Microsaurs, as well as notes about what they ate and how many of them there were, and he'd even given each of them a name.

"At first I thought it was all a joke. Most uncles, and nearly all paleontologists, are practical jokers. But the more I read his notes, the more I became convinced he was telling the truth."

"How much farther is this lab of yours?" Lin asked.

"Just over that little hill there. You'll see it any minute now," Professor Penrod said.

"So, did you go to Peru?" I asked.

"Of course. As quickly as I could, but it took me a while to find the Microsaurs. They are quite shy little creatures. Or at least they are when you're four hundred times taller than they are. Things change when you get down to their level, as you've noticed firsthand, Danny.

"I followed my uncle Penrod's map, and searched and searched for the tiny critters. No matter how hard I looked, I couldn't find a single sign of them, or of my uncle for that matter. But then I remembered something I'd learned from my old days as a bird-watcher. The best way to observe is to blend in. So, I invented and built the first Wearable Environmental Concealment Apparatus."

"The what?" I asked.

"His grass pajamas," Lin said.

"Precisely, Lin. My, you have a knack for naming things. I think grass pajamas is a much better name. I believe I'll adopt that as well."

"Thank you, I've always been good at renaming things. I even renamed my little sister ChuChu, but my parents still call her Chen. ChuChu is a much better name, if you ask me." Lin looked so proud I was afraid she would pop.

"And so the grass pajamas helped you find the Microsaurs?" I asked.

"Absolutely. While wearing my grass pajamas, I blended right in to the jungle, and before long I saw my first real-life Microsaur. A tiny pterodactyl flew by, then landed on my nose.

I was so excited I forgot how to breathe for a moment. I stayed in Peru for nearly three months, studying the little miracles in their natural habitat, but it was obvious to me that they needed my help. What was originally a remote jungle location was soon to become a high-rise apartment building. You see, another discovery had happened at the same time. Someone had found gold in the jungle hills of Peru, and a mining town had popped up nearly overnight."

"Is that why your uncle sent you the notebook? So you could go rescue the Microsaurs?" Lin asked. I had passed the leather notebook to her and she was looking through it as she walked.

"Undoubtedly, Lin. While I was never able to find my uncle Penrod, I am certain this is exactly why he sent it my way," Professor Penrod explained.

"So, what did you do? How did you get them here?" I asked.

"There weren't many of them at first. Eleven of them, to be exact. Three flyers, two sprinters,

two long-necked sauropods, a couple of grumpy stegosauri, and a pair of old triceratops, but the longer I looked the more I found. Before long, I had rounded up nearly a hundred Microsaurs."

"Bruno 2?" I asked.

"No, actually. Twoee and his two sisters were the first Microsaurs hatched in the Microterium. He's just a puppy," Professor Penrod said. Now he looked so proud I was afraid *he* was going to pop.

"I collected the gang of Microsaurs, and as much of their habitat as I could gather. Packed them up in large shipping crates, and sent the entire collection to my home here in the desert. I built the Microterium out of this old barn, invented the Shrink-A-Fier, and the rest, as they say in the movies, is history."

"Do they say that in the movies?" Lin asked, and Professor Penrod laughed.

The hill we climbed seemed to go on forever, but eventually we made it to the top. On the other side, I was surprised to see an upside-down cereal box with a hole cut in it for a door.

"Well, here we are. The Microterium Paleontological Center for the Study of Living Microsaurs," Professor Penrod said.

"Not a bad name, Professor, but I think we can do better," Lin said with a smile. She looked out over the old cereal box, then waved her hand slowly across the land. "The Fruity Stars Lab."

Professor Penrod laughed and nodded his head. "I love it. The Fruity Stars Lab it is."

Something rumbled in the jungle behind us and we all turned to look. Down at the bottom of the hill, Bruno 2 was stomping down the grass and rubble, sniffing around like a hound dog on a trail. He looked up at me, made eye contact, and I swear he looked ready to charge again.

"Um, he's looking at me like I'm lunch again, Professor Penrod," I said. My insides were rumbling, and not just because I hadn't eaten

anything since the corn dog earlier that day.

"He's not much of a climber, but we better make our way to the Fruity Stars Lab in a hurry," Professor Penrod said.

"That's not the only reason we need to hurry back. I have plans on being the Ramp-O-Saurus long-distance jumping champion in a couple of hours. It's going to be pretty hard to do that if I'm only a half-inch tall," Lin said.

I couldn't believe it, but I had been so caught up in the awesomeness of hanging out with the Microsaurs that I totally forgot about Lin's competition. I checked my smartphone. It was 2:14:49. We had exactly 1 hour and 45 minutes and 11 seconds before Lin needed to be at the top of the ramp.

"Can you unshrink us at the lab, Professor Penrod?" I asked.

"Unfortunately, without the juice, we're stuck here in the Microterium," he said. "But like they say in the movies, necessity is the mother of invention."

"Now, I know they don't say THAT in the movies," Lin said.

"What kind of juice are we talking about?" I asked.

"Battery juice, Danny. Power. We need high voltage and LOTS of it, or the three of us are trapped. For good."

# CHAPTER 9 -
## I HAVE A THEORY

"I just don't understand how we could be trapped," Lin said.

"It's simple, really. Twoee ripped apart the Particulate Matter Expander 1," Professor Penrod explained.

"The what?" I asked.

"The Expand-O-Matic 1," Lin said, once

again renaming Professor Penrod's invention. She slumped down off the dice, sliding to the floor like a rag doll. "This is sooooo frustrating. All I want to do is grow four thousand times bigger and beat B.J. Hooper in the Ramp-O-Saurus competition. Is that too much to ask?"

"If you grew four thousand times bigger, you'd be larger than that skate ramp you keep talking about. We actually only need to expand 86.274 times larger than we are now, to be exact," Professor Penrod explained. "The good news is that I've rebuilt most of the machine already." He motioned to the contraption in the middle of his lab. "But the power source has been completely destroyed. I don't know what has gotten into Twoee lately." Professor Penrod looked over at me. "Actually, it was very similar behavior to how he acted when he met you, Danny."

I looked around the room, and felt like shrinking even more. I didn't mean to change Bruno 2's behavior. I was just being me.

"Oh, don't worry, Danny. It wasn't your fault. There's something else altogether that is changing Twoee's actions. But before we can even think about finding a new power source for my Expand-O-Matic, we've got to figure out this Twoee problem. I wish we had more time to observe him, because I get a feeling the answer is so close I can almost reach out and grab it."

Right next to the professor, behind the rebuilt Expand-O-Matic 2, was the destroyed shell of the Expand-O-Matic 1. He had made the machine out of an empty cherry soda can. Sometimes rubbing my chin helps me think, so I gave it a good scratch while I tried to figure out the problem.

"So, where was the Expand-O-Matic before Twoee tore it apart?" I asked.

"It was just outside the lab, where Twoee is sitting right now," Professor Penrod said.

I looked out the door, peeking at the oversized puppy-saurus. He was sleeping in the sun, totally unaware that I was hiding inside the Fruity Stars Lab.

"You're doing that chin-rubbing thing again. What are you thinking, Danny?" Lin asked.

"I don't really know yet. Has he chewed up anything else?" I asked.

"Now that you mention it. I've been growing a few vegetables here in the Microterium, running a few experiments about reductive plant growth in a controlled environment. Very interesting stuff, I promise you that. Anyway, the other day, Twoee stomped on every ripe tomato in my garden," Professor Penrod said, and the answer to the Bruno 2 problem clicked into place like the last piece in a puzzle.

"Ha! That's it!" I shouted, which actually woke up Twoee, and he barked excitedly outside the lab. "I have a theory. Lin, are you feeling brave?"

"Pshaw. Always," she said as she stood up with a huge smile on her face.

"Okay. I need a new shirt. Professor, any chance I can borrow your grass pajama top?"

Penrod had already taken the thing off, and it was lying on a cluttered workbench.

"Certainly. I'll start cutting it down to size," he said.

"Awesome," I said. I dug to the bottom of my backpack and found a pair of scissors, then I took a deep breath. "Sorry, Dad. But I'm doing this for science." I chopped the right arm off my bright red SpyZoom T-shirt.

"What are you doing?" Lin asked.

"Hand me that wooden pole, would ya? The one propped up next to the filing cabinet," I said, and Lin helped me out. She tossed me the stick, and I tied my cut-off sleeve to the top of it, turning it into a small flag.

Professor Penrod had used a pair of scissors of his own to cut the grass pajama shirt down to my size, and he brought it over. I slipped it on over my red shirt and I was shocked by how heavy it was.

"All right, what's the plan, Dan?" Lin asked, and I handed her the flag.

"Hold this behind your back, and don't show it to Bruno 2 until I say so. I'll go out first, then you two come out after me," I said.

"Are you sure, Danny? What if Twoee charges after you again?" Professor Penrod said.

"Well then, I guess I'll need to run faster than last time. But I have a feeling he won't," I said. "Are you ready?" I asked Lin, and she nodded.

Stepping out of the Fruity Stars Lab and staring right into the face of a two-thousand-pound, three-horned Microsaur would make just about anybody nervous. My knees were wobbly and my head felt a bit dizzy as I remembered how it felt to have Bruno 2 shove me to the ground. I swallowed and tried to look as brave as Lin, but I'm pretty sure Bruno 2 didn't buy it.

"Hey, Bruno 2. How you doing, big boy?" I said, and the big triceratops tilted his head at me and gave me a little smile. Which totally surprised me, because it was a kind smile, not anything like the one he'd showed me when he was towering over me in the mud. His tongue rolled out of his mouth and he started panting. "You guys can come out now, but keep that flag hidden, Lin," I said as I held out my hand and started walking slowly toward Bruno 2.

Lin and Professor Penrod walked out of the Fruity Stars Lab and stood behind me.

"Hey, buddy, how you doing?" I asked, using my best puppy voice. "Can you sit for me?" I asked, and Bruno 2 plopped his rump in the dirt. His tail wagged, creating a dust cloud all around him.

"That's a good boy," I said as I got almost close enough to reach out and touch him. "Okay, Lin. Time to raise the flag, but be ready to throw it."

"Why?" Lin asked.

"Oh, you'll see," I said.

Lin raised the flag and the calm look in Bruno 2's eyes went all wonky. He jumped up, then began pawing the ground with his big flat foot. He made a chuffing, growling sound that I recognized from earlier, then he pounced toward the red flag that Lin held above her head.

"Throw it!" I said, but I didn't really need to. Lin had already thrown the flag-stick, and Bruno 2 turned to chase after it. He smashed it into the ground, then fell on it and chewed the thing to bits.

The three of us watched Bruno 2 roll around on the shreds of my red shirtsleeve.

"Hmm," Professor Penrod said. "Well, there goes my theory."

"What was your theory, Penny?" Lin asked.

"I always thought Microsaurs were color-blind."

After solving the Bruno 2 problem, it was time to turn our attention to an even bigger issue. The issue of getting bigger.

Professor Penrod explained how the machine worked, and I really wished that my dad was there to help. He'd know just what to do in a pinch like this.

"A purple liquid, which is a compound mixture of Burbankian cactus root oil, hydrogenated phosphorus, pomegranate amalgamate, and a small amount of grape soda, shoots through this pipe here. Then the liquid is dispersed into the air with this mister right here." He pointed to what looked like an old showerhead. "But none of that matters without the power. The real juice that makes this machine purr."

"How much power are we talking about here?

Twelve volts? A hundred? A thousand?" I asked, my eyes getting bigger with each suggestion.

"Oh no. Being the size we are now, a single volt would do the trick. The power source that Twoee destroyed was a nearly dead watch battery," Professor Penrod said.

I pulled out my phone and launched the SpyZoom app. Sometimes it helped me to focus on something entirely new for a few minutes. I don't know why it works, but it does. In fact, one time I figured out how to wire a lightbulb for my science project while mowing the lawn. It's funny how the brain works. The clock in the weather section of my SpyZoom app said is was 2:48. Just 1 hour, 12 minutes, and 14 seconds until Ramp-O-Saurus time.

"Do you think we could have Bruno 2 run in a big hamster wheel or something? I bet that would generate a volt or two," Lin suggested.

"That's a really good idea, Lin. If only we had a triceratops-sized hamster wheel," Professor Penrod said.

I was watching the GPS window in the SpyZoom app and noticed something odd. The beacon had stopped moving.

"Professor Penrod. Do you know where this is?" I showed him the little GPS map, and he studied it.

"If I'm reading this right, I'd say that it is somewhere just outside of the Microterium. Back on my lab table in my barn-lab, I'd guess," he said. "What is it, Danny?"

"It's one of my dad's inventions. It's a SpyZoom Micro-GPS Beacon. One of the pterodactyls actually brought it here. Ripped it right off Lin's helmet. We followed it to the lab. It's how we found you," I explained.

"That's right. We never found the little thief, did we, Danny?" Lin said.

"Well, we might need it now more than ever," I said.

"Why is that?" Professor Penrod said.

"Because it generates its own power. And guess how much it needs to operate?" I said with a smile. I had that awesome feeling, one of my all-time favorite feelings, the feeling that I had just solved an unsolvable problem. "Point-nine volts. Do you think that will be enough?"

"It'll have to be, won't it?" Professor Penrod said.

"Now the question is, how do we get all the way to the barn-lab, find the beacon, return to the Fruity Stars Lab, and expand 86.274 times our size in less than one hour and twelve minutes?" I asked.

"Where's a taxi when you need one?" Lin asked.

Professor Penrod raised his finger above his head and opened his eyes really wide. He was smiling as he ran to his cluttered work desk and started shuffling things around on the surface.

"What are you looking for, Professor?" Lin asked.

"This!" he said as he raised a shiny brass trumpet into the air. He ran out of the Fruity Stars Lab, leaving the cardboard door open behind him. He put his lips to the trumpet and gave it a great big BLAT!

We followed him outside. "What are you doing?" I asked.

Professor Penrod honked on the trumpet again, then smiled and looked at us.

"I'm calling us a taxi."

# CHAPTER 11
## NEW FRIENDS

I've seen a lot of drawings and paintings of the duck-billed dinosaurs. There's even a life-sized sculpture of one in the Museum of Natural History we visited on our field trip last year, but nothing prepared me for seeing the huge beast running toward Professor Penrod and his loud trumpet.

"That's Honk-Honk. She's never far away, and she's perhaps the kindest creature I've ever met," Professor Penrod said. I couldn't believe how fast she made her way to us. One minute she was wading around in a green swampy pond below the Fruity Stars Lab, and the next she was skidding to a stop right next to Professor Penrod.

"What kind of Microsaur is she?" Lin asked.

"She's a hadrosaur. Isn't she magnificent?" Professor Penrod said.

She was taller than a basketball rim: eleven, maybe even twelve feet tall. A long, curved crest stretched out from the back of her head. Her smooth, pale green skin was covered in tiny scales that made you want to run your hand down her back, and she had the kindest eyes I've ever seen.

Bruno 2 was bored waiting around, so he started chasing his tail. Professor Penrod blatted two more out-of-tune notes on his trumpet. Honk-Honk joined him and

I had to plug my ears. *HuuuuOOOOONK!*
*HuuuuuuuOOOOOOOOOOOONK!*

As she honked, the big crest on her head
vibrated and shimmered with bright patterns
of purple and green. I'd read before about other
animals that shift their colors. Chameleons can
match their environments, and some
squid flash colors in
their bodies to
communicate, but
I wasn't expecting
something this
amazing.

"Wow! That
was so cool! What
are we waiting
for?" Lin asked.
She looked like
she was ready
to climb onto

Honk-Honk and take off without us if we didn't hurry up.

"We're waiting for him," Professor Penrod said. He pointed to a dot zigzagging back and forth in the distance.

*HuuuuuOOOONK! Honk, honk!*

"Who is it?" I asked.

"His name is Zip-Zap." The speedy Microsaur was moving so fast he looked like a purple blur. He was close enough that I could see he was covered in bright purplish feathers and he had long legs and a pointed beak.

"He's so fast," Lin said.

"Yes. Riding Zip-Zap takes a very special person. A person not afraid of ninety-degree turns, unpredictable hops and jumps, and a top speed of fifty-five miles per hour."

Lin and I shared a look, then burst out laughing because we both knew that if Lin could design her own Microsaur she would make her very own Zip-Zap.

The Microsaur sprinted toward us, then glided in and stopped right next to Honk-Honk. It was easy to see that the two Microsaurs were good friends. They nuzzled together, Zip-Zap making soft cooing noises, and Honk-Honk honking quietly.

"He is the most beautiful creature I've seen in my whole life," Lin said. "Zip-Zap is so cute I can't unlook." Then, without asking if it was safe, Lin ran to Zip-Zap and threw her arms around his fluffy neck. "Can I keep him?"

Professor Penrod laughed. "You can ride him. How about we start there?"

Lin jumped and *yahooed* so loud that even Honk-Honk looked impressed. In a single bound, Lin was on Zip-Zap's back, ready to take off.

"To the POWER SOURCE!" Lin shouted, and Zip-Zap took off in the wrong direction. I could hear Lin laughing as the Microsaur ran around the place like a wild maniac.

"Um, should we tell her she went the wrong way?" I asked.

"Nah. Let her go for now. We'll have Honk-Honk call her to us when we get there." Honk-Honk raised a leg and Professor Penrod used it like a stepladder as he climbed on Honk-Honk's shoulder. "Well, it looks like Twoee is ready for you," he said.

Bruno 2 had crouched down in the grass. He barked and looked right at me. I double-checked to make sure my red shirt wasn't poking out from beneath my resized grass pajama top. I couldn't believe what was happening. Sure, I'd just seen Lin and Professor Penrod climb onto their Microsaurs, but now it was my turn. I'd never even ridden a horse before, and now I was seconds away from riding a real-life triceratops!

"I know we got off to a bad start, Bruno 2, but let's put that behind us and go find that beacon," I said, and he chuffed in agreement.

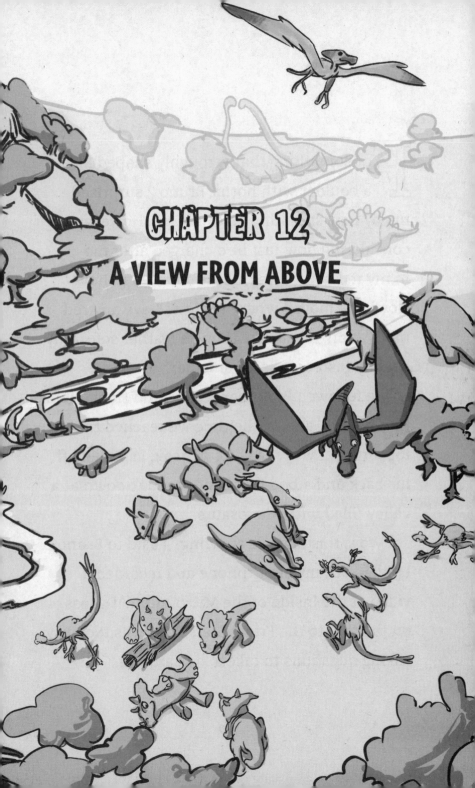

# CHAPTER 12

## A VIEW FROM ABOVE

For something that is roughly shaped like a boulder with horns, Bruno 2 surprised me by how smoothly he could run. However, considering how fast he'd charged after me in my red shirt, I was a little shocked at how slowly he moved when he didn't have any red motivation. It was like riding a leather sofa, only slightly faster and a bit smellier.

We followed Professor Penrod and Honk-Honk up a big hill, and by the time we reached the top, Bruno 2 was ready for a break. I slipped off his back and stood by his side to look down at a valley filled with Microsaurs.

"Wow, this place is amazing," I said to Bruno 2. I pulled out my smartphone and recorded a video of the inside of the Microterium. I guess on the way to the Fruity Stars Lab I was too busy asking questions to take a look around.

There was an area covered with rolling sand dunes, a swampy area with bubbling mud and odd trees, a pine forest mixed with tall grass and big flat boulders, and much more. Running in the deep grass was a herd of Microsaurs of every shape and size. There were stegosauri with plates running down their spines and spiked tails, dimetrodons with big scaly sails on their backs, and a bunch I didn't quite recognize at first, but I planned on researching each one of them when I got home.

Honk-Honk *honk*ed, and Bruno 2 jerked forward.

"Whoa, buddy. Give me a warning next time," I said as I grabbed on to his wide crest and climbed back on for the ride.

We ran down the hill and I couldn't help but laugh to myself. I tried to take a selfie with my phone, but it was so jiggly riding down the other side of the big hill on Bruno 2 that it probably looked more like the ketchup-smeared

pterodactyl from earlier. But I didn't care
because I had never been so happy in
my entire life.

Bruno 2 sloshed through the little

creek and stomped toward Professor Penrod and Honk-Honk, who were standing in the middle of the spilled desk supplies.

Honk-Honk *honk*ed and it echoed through the Microterium, and that helped. Bruno 2 picked up the speed a little.

We had almost joined Professor Penrod when a blur passed by my side, with a hollering Lin on its back. "Whoo-hooo!" she screamed, sounding like a cowgirl at the world's first Microsaur rodeo.

I slipped off Bruno 2's back, patted him on the nose, and thanked him for the ride. Then I checked my GPS tracker on the SpyZoom app. I had a pretty good idea of where the pterodactyl had taken the beacon, but I wanted a second opinion. I handed the smartphone to Professor Penrod.

"What do you think? Where should we start looking for the beacon?" I asked as I removed my backpack and dug in the bottom for a pair of binoculars.

"I believe I know two things. One, I know exactly who took your GPS beacon, and two, I know precisely where it is," Professor Penrod said.

"Oh yeah? Well then, let's go grab it and hurry back and Expand-O-Fy!" Lin said as she tried to feed Zip-Zap a fresh-picked handful of blue grass.

"Yeah. That sounds great," I said.

"Well, it won't be quite that simple. You see, the GPS beacon thief, as you call her, is none other than Twiggy. And while Twiggy is pretty good at taking directions, she does have quite a habit of stuffing shiny objects into her nest," Professor Penrod explained. "Her nest is on the third shelf up on the left, above the fish tank. Getting up there will not be easy."

"I bet Zip-Zap could get me up there. He's a pretty good jumper," Lin said, not ready to give up just yet.

Using my binoculars, I searched the area above the fish tank and found Twiggy's nest. It was filled with little trinkets and shiny things, but right in the middle, next to three pink eggs, was my dad's GPS beacon.

"Yup. I see it. But it's way too high up there. Even for Zip-Zap," I said.

"Well then, what are we going to do? We

can make a rope out of the dental floss and climb up somehow," Lin suggested. I was about to offer an idea involving making a massive slingshot out of the rubber bands and a couple of pencils, when a horrible noise interrupted my thoughts.

*EEEEEEEP!*

I looked up in the sky toward the sound and saw the bright orangish-red pterodactyl. Now that we had been Shrink-A-Fied down to his size, he looked as big as a hang glider. I couldn't help but smile as I watched him glide through the air.

Honk-Honk *honk*ed and the pterodactyl dove right toward us.

"There's your answer right there," Professor Penrod said. "Meet Twiggy. The shiny object–loving pterodactyl. And like I said, Twiggy takes directions quite well, for a Microsaur."

"Can we ride her?" Lin asked.

"I've tried, but she's not a big fan of giving rides. However, one time I did convince her to carry some supplies to the Fruity Stars Lab. All I had to do was promise her something shiny in return."

Lin dropped her skateboard to the grass, then took her helmet in her hands. She inspected it, turning it around and around in the sun. It was bright blue and as glittery as the stars in a night sky.

"Would she like this?" Lin asked. She held up the helmet and Professor Penrod smiled.

"She would, but you'll never get it back," he said.

"That's fine. If it'll help us get big, I'd give her just about anything," Lin said.

I was rubbing my chin, thinking real hard again, and Lin noticed.

"What are you thinking, Danny?" Lin asked.

"I'm thinking we need a plan, and I might

have a wild idea," I said. "Quick. Hand me that bottle cap, and, Professor, I hope you know how to tie good knots."

# CHAPTER 13
## THE PLAN

Some people at my school have teased me for carrying so much stuff in my backpack, but it doesn't worry me. I like being prepared for anything. I emptied my backpack out on the ground, and found my goggles, a pair of leather work gloves, a notebook, a calculator, and a couple of pencils and got to work.

"You see, it's pretty simple if we can build it right. Professor Penrod, you are in charge of figuring out how to steer Twiggy, and Lin and I will start working on the bottle-cap basket and harness," I said as I showed them the drawing of my plan.

Using a half-smashed tube of superglue we found in the desk rubble, Lin and I stuck four rubber bands to the bottom of a bottle cap. Then we twisted the other ends of the rubber bands in a big loop that we would need to slide over Twiggy's neck.

While we waited for the glue to dry, Professor Penrod made a bridle and some reins out of the dental floss. He said he'd been raised riding horses, and that his dad had taught him how to do it with a piece of rope.

I gave my empty backpack to Lin. She put her skateboard in it and strapped it on her back. The idea was to put the beacon inside the backpack to carry it back to the Fruity Stars Lab, and while I didn't really know why she wanted to bring along her skateboard, I did like that she wanted to be prepared as well.

I used my pocketknife to open the can of pineapple I'd packed for lunch, then I used it for something even more important than food: to trick Twiggy into walking through the rubber-band loops that Professor Penrod and Lin held up.

Everything was working as planned. We had a bottle-cap basket to ride in, a pineapple-eating pterodactyl ready to give us a ride, and I was learning how to pilot the Microsaur using the reins Professor Penrod made.

"So, pull down on the left one to go left. Then right to go right," Professor Penrod explained.

"Sounds easy," I said, really hoping that it was.

"Then let up—you know, give her a little slack—to go down, and pull back on both of the reins at the same time to go up," he said.

"Piece of cake," I said.

Lin strapped on her helmet before we climbed in the bottle-cap basket. Not only was it going to be traded for the GPS beacon, but I wanted to record the whole experience to check out later.

I gave my smartphone to Professor Penrod. I tapped on the video feed and began recording. "Okay. This is where you can see through the camera on Lin's helmet. Wave at Lin," I said to Professor Penrod. He did, and he saw himself waving on the little screen as Lin watched the two of us.

"Your dad built this?" he asked.

"Yup. You two have a lot in common," I said as I handed him the Invisible Communicator. "Now, put that inside your ear." He did without questioning me.

"Say hi, Lin," I said.

"Hi, Lin," Lin said, trying to be funny. It worked, because Professor Penrod laughed as her voice spoke inside his head using the SpyZoom Invisible Communicator.

"Now you can talk to Lin and she can talk back. Just talk normally—you don't need to shout," I said.

Twiggy was getting restless, flapping her wings and hopping around. "Come on, Danny, she's ready to go," Lin said.

"All right. Back in a few minutes with our power source!" I said, then I ran and jumped in the bottle cap.

"Bye, Professor," Lin said. She handed me the reins. I gave them a shake, and Twiggy took off like a dino-rocket.

From our new viewpoint way up in the air, the Microterium looked small once again. Even Honk-Honk and Bruno 2 looked little from inside the bottle-cap basket. It wasn't as smooth as I had imagined, because every time Twiggy flapped her wings, the whole basket rocked like a tiny boat on a wild ocean. At first, I was too excited to remember I was afraid of heights, but that wore off pretty quickly and I started getting a little queasy.

"This is incredible, Danny. Can you believe

we're doing this?" Lin said. She didn't look air-sick at all. In fact, she looked like she was going to start glowing with happiness any second.

I nodded. Sure, it was pretty cool, but I wasn't sure I wanted to talk about it just yet.

"So, the plan is, you will fly Twiggy right up to her nest, then I'll jump out and swap my helmet for the GPS beacon. Then you'll fly back around and I'll jump in the basket. Right?"

I nodded my head again, and the nodding motion added to the bobbing motion of the flying basket—plus, the fact that we were WAY up high in the air did it. I was officially airsick.

I tried to focus on deep breaths and piloting Twiggy toward the nest when . . .

¡TWANG!

The back rubber-band loop that was keeping us balanced snapped, and Lin almost slipped off the back of the bottle cap as it tipped up like the bed of a dump truck. She grabbed one of the three remaining rubber bands and kept her balance.

"That wasn't cool, Danny," she said.

I totally agreed. Not cool at all. The wind was rushing fast, and I yanked back on the reins, bringing Twiggy up even higher. We flew over the big metal step that triggered the Shrink-A-Fier turning on, and continued to soar up and up toward the fish tank.

"Professor wants to know if we're all right," Lin said. I swallowed hard, then just before I shouted back to Lin that we were going to be fine, something happened to change my mind.

Another of the rubber-band straps broke.

Lin yelped a little, and fell to her knees to try to get stable in the wobbly bottle-cap basket. "No, we're not all right," Lin shouted into the SpyZoom Invisible Communicator. "But we're almost there."

Lin and I had a rule. It had been with us since we became friends three years ago when her family moved to my neighborhood. You don't turn back on an adventure. But for the first time in those three years, I was starting to think that was a dumb rule. Really dumb. I could see the nest just ahead, but I made the mistake of looking down and I got so dizzy I felt like I would pass out any second.

"It's the bottle cap. The metal is so sharp it's sawing through the rubber bands," Lin said to me and Professor Penrod. "We have to hurry, Danny, or these are all going to snap."

I pulled on the right rein, and we dipped to the right. Lin slid from one side of the bottle cap to the other, catching herself just before she fell over the edge.

We flew past the first shelf, then we came eye to eye with the snail-squid in the fish tank. When we were regular-sized, the fish thing didn't look all that scary, but now that it was about ten times bigger than us it was downright terrifying.

"It looks like a kraken from that pirate movie we saw on your birthday," Lin said. A shiver ran down, then sprinted back up my whole body, but Lin looked like she was having the time of her life. I didn't dare open my mouth to respond. I was doing everything in my power to hold it together. I kept pulling back on the reins, steering Twiggy up higher and higher until we were gliding over the fish tank.

The third rubber band broke, and we were balanced on one single rubber band. I looked down and the top of the fish tank looked like an Olympic-sized swimming pool as we kept flying up toward the nest.

I could feel the sickness creeping up in my throat, and I was afraid it was going to join us in the bottle-cap basket. Twiggy flapped three more times, and there it was: the shiny metal GPS beacon, tucked away in her nest.

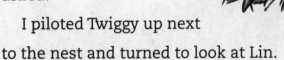

Lin saw it, too, and she tightened the straps on my backpack. "How close can you get me?" Lin asked.

I piloted Twiggy up next to the nest and turned to look at Lin.

"Take Twiggy back to Professor Penrod. I'll skate back down there," she said. She gave me a thumbs-up, smiled, launched herself off the

back of the teetering bottle cap, and landed right in the middle of Twiggy's nest.

I leaned hard to the left, turning Twiggy back around. Then, just when I had gotten my balance, my biggest fear came true.

The last rubber band sprang, and the bottle cap fell out from beneath my feet. I held on tight to the reins, dangling over the floor of the barn-lab-library. The noise and me wiggling around made Twiggy go a little wild, and she spun around and started soaring toward the workbench on the other side of the barn-lab. The good news was that I was suddenly so terrified that I would fall to my death, that I totally forgot to be airsick.

I held on as long as I could, but my hands were sweaty from all the excitement, and no matter what I did I could not keep my grip on the waxy dental-floss reins. "Aaarrrrgh!" I shouted. I tumbled through the air, spinning around and around as I fell like a stone toward the hard wooden floor. I know it is a strange thing to think about when you're falling through the sky, but I wished that I had packed my dad's antigravity sleeping bag. The wind was shouting in my ears as I fell, and I closed my eyes as

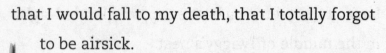

the floor came rushing faster and faster toward me. Or, I guess, more accurately, it was me that was rushing toward it. Then less than a second before I was splatted flat, Twiggy came to my rescue.

Nothing could have prepared me for the feeling of two long, clawed talons ripping through my grass pajama top and the back of my red SpyZoom T-shirt.

She saved me just in time, then flapped her massive wings and the two of us soared back up into the sky.

The relief of not being turned into a Danny puddle rushed over me, and I laughed and shouted with joy as Twiggy and I glided through the air. Not a trace of airsick remained, just pure happiness as the wind rushed through my hair.

Honk-Honk *honked*, and Twiggy turned her head, tucked her wings, and dive-bombed toward the honking Microsaur. In less than a minute, she was dropping me off on the ground next to Professor Penrod, then she was on her way, flying off into the air.

"Are you all right, Danny?" Professor Penrod asked. He looked like he'd seen a ghost.

He helped me up and
I nodded my head,
because I thought that
I actually was all right,
although I wasn't 100
percent sure.

"Is Lin okay?" I asked.

"Ask her yourself," Professor Penrod said

as he passed me the SpyZoom Invisible
Communicator and my smartphone.

"Lin. Are you okay?" I asked. She turned the
camera toward her face and looked right back
at me.

"Never better. I pried the camera out of my
helmet; I hope that's okay. I just traded my
old skate helmet for a GPS beacon lodged in
a pterodactyl's nest," Lin said into the Invisible
Communicator. "I can't believe I just said that
sentence. What a day, right?"

"You can say that again," I said. "So you
grabbed the beacon?" I asked.

The video bobbled around a little as Lin
fidgeted with the straps of my backpack.
"Check it out!" Lin had not only gotten the GPS
beacon, but she had already stuffed it in the
backpack.

"So, give us a time check, Danny," Lin said.

The battery was running low on my smartphone,

but the clock said it was 3:18. "We have exactly forty-two minutes and twelve seconds."

"Well then, I guess I better get going. Hold on to your guts!" Lin said. She looked down and I watched as she put her skateboard on top of the long wooden ruler she'd propped up against the shelf. "Hey, Danny. Do you think this is longer than the Ramp-O-Saurus?"

I looked down the ramp she'd built. It was at least twice as long as the Ramp-O-Saurus, but I didn't have time to tell her because she jumped onto the ramp and started skating down.

Professor Penrod watched through the binoculars while I viewed the video feed from the little wireless camera Lin held in her hand. The ruler was so slick that Lin got up to full speed in less than a second. I took a glance at the SpyZoom app, and the GPS beacon in her backpack registered that she was moving 30.2 miles per hour. A personal BEST!

I didn't realize I was holding my breath until Lin reached the bottom. I'd never seen her move so fast as she zipped across the top of an old filing cabinet, grinding on the edge just for fun. She kick-flipped off the filing cabinet, launching herself over a huge gap. She really did fly for a second or two before her wheels touched down on a ladder leaning against the wall. She rode the ladder all the way down to the metal step

below
the
Shrink-A-Fier,
then her momentum
burst toward the red-and-
white straw that brought us to the
Microterium in the first place. She didn't
even stop at the lip of the straw, she just ollied
over the edge and zoomed down the big red-
and-white pipe, and came skidding to a stop a
few feet away from me and Professor Penrod.

"That was CRAZY COOL, Lin! Seriously, the
most amazing thing I've ever seen. And I have it
ALL on video! You are going to be a star when we
put this online. Holy golden corn dogs! That . . .
was . . . AWESOME!"

I jumped around and shouted. Soon Zip-Zap was running a big circle around all of us and Bruno 2 was stomping up a dirt cloud. Even Professor Penrod got into the act as he did a little shuffling dance thing that made him look older than he actually was.

Lin ran up to us, nearly out of breath. "Okay . . . how . . . long did . . . that take?" she said between gasps of air.

I checked my smartphone. "We have thirty-four minutes and thirty-one seconds left. But that was *soooo* cool!" I said again. I couldn't help shouting.

"Okay, okay. It was cool." Lin swallowed, then took one last deep breath to get back to normal. "But we need to get to back to the Fruity Stars Lab in a hurry. And I have an idea."

"Oh yeah? What's that?" I asked.

"Well, let's just say I'm going to need your other shirtsleeve," Lin said with a smile.

# CHAPTER 14
## THE EXPAND-O-MATIC 2

Professor Penrod got a head start on Honk-Honk, rushing back to prepare the Expand-O-Matic as Lin and I worked on her genius plan.

It was simple, really, as most genius plans are. First, Lin distracted Bruno 2 while I cut off my other sleeve. Then it was my turn to distract Bruno 2 with some serious belly rubbing, while Lin tied shirt scraps to Zip-Zap's tail feathers.

"If we keep going like this, I won't have any shirt left," I said to Lin when she climbed onto Zip-Zap.

"Don't worry. This is going to work. You'll get to keep what's left of your shirt for yourself," she said.

I climbed onto Bruno 2 for the second time that day, then Lin whistled to get his attention.

Zip-Zap played along perfectly, wiggling his tail feathers and waving the red T-shirt scraps back and forth. Lin steered Zip-Zap back to the Fruity

Stars Lab, and I held on for my life as Bruno 2 showed me what triceratops top-speed felt like. At first it was a bit too bumpy for me to enjoy, but eventually I got used to the running rhythm, and for the first time ever I understood exactly why Lin loved riding her skateboard so fast. Zip-Zap and Lin darted, ducked, and jumped over, under, and around trees and bushes. Bruno 2 took a more direct approach, smashing right through the very same trees and bushes Zip-Zap had avoided.

When we arrived back at the Fruity Stars Lab, we left the Microsaurs outside, where Bruno 2 continued to chase Zip-Zap around the lab. We rushed inside to find Professor Penrod. There was black grease on his hands, his shirt, and smeared across his forehead, but he looked excited when he saw that Lin had the GPS beacon strapped to her back.

"How much time to do we have, Danny?" Lin asked.

I checked my watch. "Oh man. We've got to hurry. That took longer than I thought. We only have nine minutes."

"That's fine, really. This will only take a second, and the skate park is, what, three minutes, four minutes from my house? You'll be back in time to grab a deep-fried candy bar or something," Professor Penrod said as he pulled the GPS beacon from the backpack. I took off what was left of the grass pajama top and put it on the workbench.

"So, what do we do next?" I asked.

"Simple. I'll get this cranked up, and you two need to step outside. There's a little square piece of copper behind the lab. Stand on it and wait to be unshrunk," he said with a confident smile.

He used a glop of what looked like tree sap to stick an old wire to the top of the GPS beacon, then he held the other end of the wire in his hand. "As soon as I connect this, it'll start right up. Head outside. And let's do this again, what do you say?" he offered, and I was so excited I might have replied too loudly.

"YES! PLEASE! We'd love to come back," I shouted.

"Can we come back tomorrow?" Lin asked.

"Ha. We'll see each other soon enough. That's a promise," Professor Penrod said. "Now, quickly. Out on the copper circle, and what was it that Lin said earlier? Oh yes. Hold on to your guts."

We ran outside and stood on the copper slab, which I realized was a shiny penny.

Bruno 2 was so busy chasing Zip-Zap around that he didn't even notice I was standing in the open in my red shirt. It probably didn't really matter anyway, because it was covered in mud, ripped to shreds, had two huge claw holes in the back, and was totally stretched out. I was a mess, but it was totally worth it.

"All right, you two. Here goes," Professor Penrod shouted from inside.

Lin and I both jumped a little as we heard the loud ZAP. Then a crinkly, fizzly sound came next, followed by a loud BOOM and a crash that sounded like someone had tipped over a stack of dishes.

We stood there for a moment, but nothing happened.

"Did we unshrink?" Lin asked.

"Um, no. We're still microsized," I said.

The back door to the Fruity Stars Lab creaked open, and Professor Penrod tumbled out. His hair and cheeks were covered in black soot and one of his glasses lenses was cracked.

"I'm sorry, you two. But I'm afraid I have bad news. The wiring that hooked the GPS beacon to the Expand-O-Matic 2 was a bit too chewed on and it shorted out."

"So we can't go back?" Lin asked.

The professor shook his head and looked down at his feet. "I'm so sorry," he said.

"Ever?" Lin asked. Her voice sounded a bit worried. I looked at the smartphone I held in my hand, and I had the spark of a little idea.

"Oh, I'm sure we'll solve this problem, too. I mean, look what the three of us have already accomplished today. It's been a miracle, to say the least. If we put our heads together, I'm sure we can get us back to normal size before long," Professor Penrod said.

"But not in eight minutes," Lin said. I looked over at her and she swallowed real hard. Of all the things I'd seen that day, this might have been the most amazing, because Lin was about to cry. And that made me feel like crying, too, but the little spark of an idea came back and a tiny bit of hope pushed away any tears.

I turned the phone over in my hands and I could see a little scrape where my dad had used a screwdriver to pry the back off. He'd opened it up and shown me how to swap out the phone's graphics processor chip with a faster one. I still remember what he said when he did it.

*"This could wipe out all the memory, so make sure you back up the videos or any pictures you have on the phone before you monkey with it like this."*

*"So, what you're saying is it's okay to monkey with it?"*

*"Well, let's try to keep this one all in one piece.*

*It's a*
*prototype. A one*
*of a kind. But it's good to*
*know HOW to monkey with*
*something like this if you ever need to."*

I wasn't sure I wanted to do it. I mean, if
I lost all the amazing video I'd captured that
day, I'd never get it back. It's not every day that
you get to ride on the back of a triceratops and
hang out as a half-inch-tall kid with a bunch of

Microsaurs. But in the end, getting Lin back in time was more important than anything else. So I took a deep breath and pried the back of my dad's old smartphone off with my fingernail. I studied the circuitry and processors hidden behind the chrome phone case. Wrapped around all the fancy parts inside the phone were two long wires, one red and one blue.

"What are you doing, Danny?" Lin asked. "Don't ruin your phone. We'll find another way."

I checked the time one last time before I zapped my phone for good. "Not in six minutes and twenty-one seconds we won't," I said. I threw the smartphone to Professor Penrod.

"How much wire do you need?" I asked Professor Penrod.

"Not much. Just a couple of small pieces ought to do," Professor Penrod said.

"Get us back, Professor Penrod. Lin's got a trophy to win," I said.

# CHAPTER 15

## CRUSHING IT ON THE RAMP-O-SAURUS

"Well, skate fans, we're down to the last two competitors. The two you've all been waiting for," the announcer boomed through the speakers at my back. The crowd shouted and I cheered right along with them, my dad by my side.

"I know it's hard to believe, Dad. Impossible, even, but I promise it is the truth. Every word. And I have the shirt to prove it," I said. My dad might be the most forgiving and understanding person on planet Earth, but even he has his limits. I mean, who would ever believe the day that Lin and I had had? And without my smartphone video to prove it, I really couldn't blame him.

"Well, your shirt is a mess. That's for sure," he said. He ruffled my hair and gave me his best half smile, but it didn't help.

I felt like I had let him down a little. He didn't believe me, I could see it on his face. "Come on. Let's enjoy the show and worry about the details later."

"Next up is B.J. Hooper, last year's champion. B.J. is trying to make the best of this jump, because this is his last year competing in the Under-12 Ramp-O-Saurus Long Distance Jumping Contest as he turns twelve in just a few days." The crowd started chanting, "B.J.! B.J.! B.J.!" but I didn't join in. There was no way I was going to root for him when he was trying to beat my best friend.

"Hey, I have an idea, Dad. I could take you to the Microterium. We could shrink down and you could meet Professor Penrod and see the Microsaurs for yourself," I said.

My dad was clapping for B.J. because he's a nice guy, and he raised an eyebrow. "Hmm. Well, if you think that will work, I'd be up for a trip like that," he said, but I could tell he still didn't believe me.

I just didn't feel right inside. Even though he wouldn't come right out and say it, my dad thought I made up the whole Microsaur story to explain how I lost his smartphone prototype and the SpyZoom Micro-GPS Beacon. And to make things worse, I couldn't talk to Lin with our SpyZoom Invisible Communicators, because without the smartphone and the app, they were nothing more than tiny earplugs.

I looked up at Lin. After leaving her old helmet in Twiggy's nest, she had to use her backup helmet. It was purple, with a row of spikes, which seemed perfect after our day with the Microsaurs. She looked no bigger than she had in the Microterium as she waited on top of the Ramp-O-Saurus. I don't know how she felt, but if she was as nervous and tired as me, I wondered how she was even going to compete. I hoped she had enough energy left to teach B.J. Hooper a lesson.

The crowd roared, bringing me out of my daydream.

"Another perfect jump by Hooper. You're looking at your new leader! B.J. Hooper has just set a world-record jump with a distance of sixty-five feet, four inches!" the announcer said. Skate fans from around the world cheered as the news was broadcast on live TV.

"Not bad," my dad said as he clapped along. "A new world record. How about that, Danny."

I looked up at him and smiled on the outside, but on the inside I was worried. That was until I looked up to the top of the Ramp-O-Saurus. I expected to see Lin hanging her head, or looking bummed out: sixty-five feet, four inches was an impossible distance. But she wasn't sad at all. In fact, she was cheering louder than anyone in the entire crowd. She pumped her arms and pointed to the bottom of the ramp. She was giving someone the thumbs-up sign, and I looked in the foam pit to see B.J. Hooper give it back.

I was really missing the SpyZoom app now. I wished I had my Invisible Communicator more than ever so I could ask Lin how she was feeling.

"Did you see that, Dad?" I asked. "Lin was cheering for B.J. like she was his biggest fan."

"I did see that. That's a good sign, isn't it?" he said.

"What? That she's cheering on the new world champion?"

"Yeah. It tells me that she's confident that he won't be the world champ for long," he said. Then he cheered in his booming voice. "Come on, Lin! Time to fly!"

"All right, everyone, it's time for our last

challenger. Lin Song, are you ready?" the announcer asked, and Lin put her skateboard on the lip of the Ramp-O-Saurus. She nodded her head and the crowd totally shocked me because they didn't cheer at all. In fact, it was so quiet you could hear

the cotton candy machines in the background whirling around and around.

Lin shook

all the nerves out of her arms and fingers, took a deep breath, then stepped on the front of her skateboard. The only thing you could hear was the sound of her wheels rumbling down the wooden back of the Ramp-O-Saurus.

She tucked in so tight that even the wind couldn't find her to slow her down. Then just as she reached the bottom of the ramp, she crouched even farther.

The crowd exploded with cheers as she flew off the tail end of the ramp and opened her arms wide. She soared just like Twiggy, graceful and easy as if she belonged in the sky. I couldn't see her face from where I stood in the crowd, but that didn't matter. Every inch of her was smiling, I could just tell.

No flips. No fancy tricks. Just the most perfect glide you've ever seen, as she sailed right past B.J. Hooper's marker and dove headfirst into the foam pit.

My dad and I both jumped and shouted at the same time, joining in with the rest of the crowd as we realized that she had just won the Ramp-O-Saurus Long Distance Jumping Contest. It was pure craziness all around, people jumping up and down and chanting her name.

We cheered until our voices stopped

working. It was the perfect ending to the perfect day. Well, almost. If only I could convince Dad that I was telling the truth, but I knew that it was impossible without actually showing him.

"How about a corn dog, Danny? You look like you could use a bite to eat," my dad said, and he was right.

"Forget the dog. I could eat a whole corn brontosaurus," I said, and he laughed.

We found a table away from the noise and sat and chatted about my dad's new invention while we ate our corn dogs. He had one, and I had two, which was actually my third and fourth for the day. I was about to tell him more about the Microterium, when Lin and her family walked our way. Lin's dad was carrying her skateboard, and her little sister was wearing her helmet so that Lin could carry her new trophy.

It was almost as tall as she was. But what shocked me the most was that they had a special guest. Someone I did NOT expect to see. It was Professor Penrod, and he was carrying a large leather suitcase that was covered in stickers from around the world.

My dad saw them, too, and he turned and held out a hand. "Let me shake the hand of a world record holder! Congrats, Lin. That was the coolest thing I've ever seen on a skateboard."

"It was pretty impressive, but you should have seen what she did earlier today. Made that jump look like a little skip. Am I right?" Professor Penrod said.

"That's right," I said as I stood up fast. All the tiredness from the day washed away because I knew that the professor could explain to my dad that my story was totally, 100 percent true.

"Now, I can't stay. In fact, I'm leaving the country for a while. But I did want to give you this, Danny. You left it behind in the lab," he said with a wink. He handed me the smartphone and the GPS beacon, which was no bigger than an apple seed now that we were back to normal size. I handed the smartphone to my dad so he could see that it was in one piece.

"You're leaving?" Lin asked. "But who's going to take care of the Microsaurs?"

"I was hoping the two of you would stop by and check in on them from time to time. Maybe peanut butter up a couple of sticks for Twooee. Take Zip-Zap for a spin. You know, give the Microsaurs what they need most. Love and attention."

"What are Microsaurs?" Lin's parents asked at the same time.

"I'll tell you all about it later. Believe me, you're going to want to sit down to hear this one. You, too, ChuChu," Lin said as she pinched her two-year-old sister's cheek. Her sister made

some nonsense word that sounded like "flape-blorp," and Lin laughed because she understood her perfectly.

"I left an explanation on your device, Danny. It's right there with all the other videos from today," Professor Penrod said.

"They survived?" I said, totally shocked. I couldn't believe it. I was sure they were destroyed when Professor Penrod used the wiring to send us back through the Expand-O-Matic.

"Every last one of them," Professor Penrod said. "Well, I'm off. I have a plane to catch. Give Twoee a snuggle for me, would you? Oh, and no more red shirts, for goodness' sake."

"We're on it, Professor Penrod. Don't worry about a thing," I said. Trusting Lin and me with the Microsaurs was a big thing—huge, actually—but I knew we'd be up for the challenge.

"Travel safe, Penny," Lin said as he disappeared into the crowd. "Bring me back a toy!" she shouted after him.

"Do you know what time it is, Danny?" Lin's mom asked.

"No, but I can find out," I said, and she grinned.

"Oh, I know what time it is," Lin said as she leaned against her new trophy.

"I think I know what time it is, too," Lin's dad said. "Let me check." He rolled up his sleeve and looked at his bare wrist. He wasn't even wearing a watch, but that didn't matter because even I had figured it out, too.

"It's celebration time, isn't it?" I said.

"That's right," Lin said. "Time to eat our weight in ice cream. Do you guys want to come?"

"Can we, Dad?" I asked as I looked up at him. But my dad didn't answer. He sat back down at the table with his eyes wide and his mouth hanging open. "Are you okay?"

"I think so, but I may need to watch this again later," he said. He was holding the smartphone. He'd just finished watching a video of me, his only son, being chased by a triceratops. "I think I just saw a real, live dinosaur."

"It was a Microsaur, actually, and just wait until you see Twiggy. That's when things get really crazy," I said, then I ruffled his hair and gave him a half smile. "Come on, Dad. It looks like you need some ice cream, too."

# A VIDEO NOTE FROM PROFESSOR PENROD

"Is this working?" Professor Penrod said as he tapped the screen with his finger. "I hope so. I'm not so good with new technology. I prefer the old stuff, if I'm being honest."

He sat back and cleared his throat. Bruno 2 was still chasing Zip-Zap and they zoomed by the professor in the background.

"Danny and Lin. Today's adventures were the second-best thing I've experienced all year. And considering that I discovered the Microsaurs this year, that is saying a lot. For some time I've been looking for someone to take care of the Microsaurs while I go out in the field and search for more, but the right person has not come along until now.

"Today's events were a test of sorts. A test I didn't know was necessary until it was underway. I realize it was a bit risky at times, but it looked like you two enjoyed it as much as I did. You two are brilliant. Adventurous, smart, and dare I say fearless! You followed Twiggy to the barn. You discovered the note in the microscope. You even figured out the clues I left behind on how to enter the Microterium.

You two managed every step and obstacle in the way with creativity, brain power, and bravery. It's exactly the type of team I need to help me grow the Microterium."

He smiled to himself as he remembered something. "Oh, and discovering what it was that was driving Twoee crazy: the color red—I never would have guessed. Just brilliant, Danny. You have the makings of a great scientist, that is for sure."

He held up the leather notebook no bigger than a wallet. "Remember this? It's the notebook sent to me by my uncle Penrod. It's the one that led me to Peru to find the Microsaurs. Well, there's something I didn't show you. Here, let me just take you back inside the Fruity Stars Lab with me," Professor Penrod said. He picked up the camera and the video got all wobbly for a minute while he walked inside the lab. He focused the camera on a small bookshelf. There were five little leather notebooks stacked in a row.

"What I didn't show you at the time is that the Peru notebook was one of six notebooks sent to me that day. Each from a new area of the world where my uncle had discovered more Microsaurs. I couldn't bear to leave my Microterium unattended while I searched for the others, but now that you two are around, I think it's time for me to go exploring once again. Who knows, perhaps I'll find Uncle Penrod as well.

"But there is one thing I need you two to do that we haven't discussed. I need you to keep the Microterium a secret. Sure, it is fine that your parents know. Parents should always know things of this importance. But that's it. Nobody else can know about the Microterium. For the safety of Bruno 2, Zip-Zap, Honk-Honk, Twiggy, and all the other Microsaurs, it's very important that we keep it a secret for now. I'm sure you will understand."

He pulled one of Uncle Penrod's notebooks from the shelf and opened it up.

"Let's see. Where to next." He thumbed through a few pages, then his eyes opened wide and a big smile crossed his face. "Looks like I'm heading to China. Take care, Danny and Lin. And remember, adventure awaits!"

# FACTS ABOUT PTEROSAURS

- There's no such thing as a pterodactyl. Nobody knows exactly when people started calling the flying dinosaurs pterodactyls (which means "winged finger" by the way), but it's more of a nickname than an actual name. The name came from the family name of the pterosaurs, and there were hundreds of different types of pterosaurs. Perhaps even THOUSANDS!

- If you think pterodactyl (tear-a-DACK-til) is hard to pronounce, wait until you try to find out who Twiggy really is. She's a pterosaur, for sure, but specifically she is a *Quetzalcoatlus* (KWET-zal-koh-AT-lus). *Quetzalcoatlus* were massive, with wingspans of more than thirty feet, and they were taller than giraffes!

- At first, Professor Penrod wondered why Twiggy was so attracted to shiny objects, but after researching her ancestors, the pterosaurs, it all made sense. Many pterosaurs were fish eaters, and silvery fish scales were perhaps the shiniest thing around over sixty-five million years ago.

- Don't let the wings fool you. Most birds today are descended from feather-covered, two-legged theropods, like Zip-Zap, not from flying dinosaurs. In fact, the pterosaurs are actually more closely related to today's modern alligators than to birds.

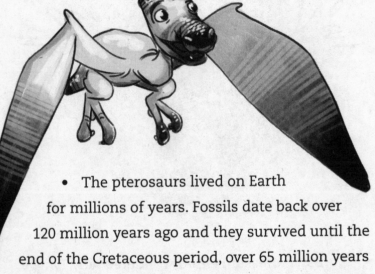

- The pterosaurs lived on Earth for millions of years. Fossils date back over 120 million years ago and they survived until the end of the Cretaceous period, over 65 million years ago. They also ranged in size more than most typical dinosaur families. The smallest was no bigger than a small sparrow and we know that the largest was the size of a small airplane.

- The smallest pterosaur fossil found so far is only about ten inches wide. Scientists have proved that it was just a baby but, believe it or not, it could already FLY!

- And last, pterosaurs were not technically dinosaurs! They were actually reptiles that lived millions of years ago. One easy way to tell the difference is that dinosaur legs extend below their bodies; take a look at Bruno 2, Honk-Honk, and Zip-Zap for examples. But pterosaurs legs and wings grow out from the sides of their bodies, more like lizard legs do today.

# ACKNOWLEDGMENTS

There's an old saying, that it takes a village to write a book. Okay, I'm twisting that saying up a little to suit my needs, but it still holds true. Actually, having just my name on the front of this book is kind of silly, because so many people had a hand in making this happen.

Annie, who told me that Honk-Honk honking was more fun than Honk honking. Making her laugh is the sunshine in my life, so—Honk became Honk-Honk.

Malorie, who loves everything I create, from the first goofy sketches of Danny with glasses and frizzy hair, to the very last drawing of Professor Penrod waving good-bye (for now).

Davis, who has become my never-ending wellspring of wild ideas, crazy pseudoscientific Microsaur names, and dinosaur memes. Lots of memes. OH so many memes.

Tanner, for being a constant companion and critiquing me like a pro. Not only is he my personal in-house Art Director and DJ, he's always there for me when I need a thirty-minute Rocket League break. Okay, who am I kidding. It's a one-hour break. Maybe two. Perhaps three on the weekends.

Ben Brooks, who never let me give up this crazy writing thing. From first drafts of books that are better left unread, through the query minefield, to publication, he's always been there to laugh, encourage, and complain. All of which play their part. You're next, Ben.

The team at Feiwel & Friends, for taking a chance

on unknown me. I'm humbled so many of you worked behind the scenes, without the credit you deserve, to turn this story into a book. But I'd be a fool not to thank Jean Feiwel for the trust, and certainly Liz Dresner for the incredible design.

Holly West, the finest editor I could ever imagine. She gets my stories and she gets ME, which is no small task. Not only does she allow me to be my creative self, she demands it. Her passion for all things tiny was the fuel in a tired author/illustrator's tank.

Gemma Cooper, my agent, my friend. Part cheerleader, part therapist, part confidante, part editor, part brainstormer, part visionary—all heart. Impossible to imagine working in the world of words without Gemma by my side.

But most of all, and forever, my dear wife, Jodi, who has read millions of my sloppy words in the past ten years. And I'm not kidding. MILLIONS. Nobody in the world understands how the two of us work, but we do, in the very best of ways. Ours is a story written in the stars, baby. This book, and all the rest, belong to you. It's me and you against the world!

# HOW TO DRAW A TINY-CERATOPS!

Ingredients
1 candy corn
1 spotted jelly bean
5 macaroni noodles

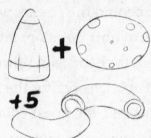

Combine the ingredients, adding the jelly bean first, then the candy corn. Add a noodle for each leg and one for the tail.

jelly bean spots are optional

Next, make the tail noodle pointy, add some ripples to the top of the candy corn, a nostril, and a dot for the eye.

Finish up with some details such as horns, a smile, a few wrinkles. Oh . . . and an eye. Don't forget the eyes!

Finally, color them however you like. If you ask me, the wilder the better!

# TWIGGY'S TERMS

```
P Y Q Y P N Q M I V H F E F J
S A H O N K H O N K R V R V E
Y X E C G W Y V X L N C U X M
Y S I N S G D N M O Y X T O I
L V T E I Z J Q N J G S N A C
U X C W M L U L R A G M E O R
K N U E I M O K Y E D I V C O
V B J Y P G K G N E U S D Q T
C L Z O A U G N I O C H A B E
S I Z I W G T Y T W J R S L R
Z P U N K C Y Q L T T I C B I
U L Q J J D O R N E P N D W U
R S K A T E B O A R D K T U M
O E S P Y Z O O M H Q N X O T
V C R A M P O S A U R U S H Y
```

| | |
|---|---|
| ADVENTURE | SHRINK |
| DANNY | SKATEBOARD |
| HONKHONK | SPYZOOM |
| LIN | TINY |
| MICROTERIUM | TWIGGY |
| PENROD | TWOEE |
| RAMPOSAURUS | |

# HELP TWIGGY FIND HER NEST!

# GO FISH

## DUSTIN HANSEN

**When did you realize you wanted to be a writer?
Or an artist?**
I honestly can't remember a time that I didn't think of myself
as an artist. Drawing, painting, sculpting, and animation are
just a part of me. But to me, art is just another way to tell a
story. I LOVE telling stories, but I didn't start writing down my
stories until I had kids of my own. So, I guess I was about
thirty days old when I became an artist (I might be exaggerating), and thirty years old when I became a writer (I may be
exaggerating here as well, but not by much).

**You write AND illustrate your books. Do you start with
the story or with the art? Which one is harder?**
Every story, book, or illustration I create begins with a question. For example, what if the dinosaurs didn't go extinct?
What if they evolved by shrinking so tiny that nobody noticed
them? A question like this leads to more questions, which leads
to a little bit of doodling, and maybe a bit of sketch-writing
(really sloppy writing to capture ideas). It is hard to say what
comes first, the art or the writing, because they both kind of
pop up together in my mind. But starting with a fun question to
answer is always the start of a good story.

**Lin is an amazing skateboarding athlete. Did you play sports as a kid?**

Oh boy, did I. I had a black Makaha long board and miles of sidewalks at the junior college near my home. Back then it was more about speed than backside 180 kickflips, but I still love that feeling of gliding a few inches above the pavement. I also loved BMX—I could go on for months about this—and playing basketball. In fact, I'm still a big NBA junkie and I never miss the X-Games.

**Who is your favorite fictional character?**

In the Microsaurs, it has to be Bruno. I know, I know, it should probably be Lin or Danny, but come on, Bruno's basically a big, lovable, puppy-saurus. If he had ears, I'd totally scratch behind them and I'd do just about anything to give him a big belly rub. He's a lot of fun to write because of his "red" thing, which causes loads of problems, and he is also a blast for me to draw.

**Danny really admires Professor Penrod. As a young person, who did you look up to most?**

Well, my parents were pretty amazing. My dad was a musician and my mom was a costume designer, so they totally understood my creative brain and inspired me to follow my dreams. There were others, of course, a wonderful art teacher named Mrs. Criner, an entomology teacher in college we called Dr. Bugs, and a writing buddy named Jamie Ford, but my parents take the cake.

**How did you celebrate publishing your first book?**

I smashed a few thousand zombies, recovered a sunken treasure, won the Super Bowl, ran away from a forest fire, and solved a series of mysterious mind puzzles on an uninhabited island. No, seriously!

My first published book, *Game On!*, was about video game history, so after a couple of fun parties to introduce my book to my friends and family, I took two weeks off and, yup, you guessed it, I played a LOT of video games.

## What's the best advice you have ever received about writing?

Without a doubt, it was that writing is like drawing. You have to sketch, gather references and research, sketch again, doodle, dream, sketch again, and probably sketch AGAIN, before you are really ready to start a final illustration. Writing is just like this. You need to try a few things, slap down a few pages of sloppy stuff, read someone else's book, write a few more throw-away pages, make some really nice mistakes, then set it all aside and start over. It's a process I call sketch-writing, and it's super effective for me. Nobody writes a perfect sentence the first time. I guess it boils down to this: It's okay to make mistakes. In fact, it's important.

## If you were a superhero, what would your superpower be?

Unlimited Energy-Man! I'd be able to draw, write, skateboard, fish, watch TV, swim, sing, hang out with friends and family, and then save a kitten from a tree without ever getting tired. I'd never stop! Maybe I'd be Never Stop Man! That would be AWESOME!

## What was your favorite thing about school?

Actually, this might be a shocker, but science. Sure, I loved art and creative writing, but I loved learning about science and the lessons science teaches about the scientific process. I especially loved biology and geology, because birds and rocks are cool. Especially when they meet and are frozen in time for 65 million years or so.

## What sparked your imagination to create the Microsaurs?

Believe it or not, I was in the hospital when I got the idea for the Microsaurs. I was all alone, a little bored, sitting in a hospital bed with tubes stuck in my arms, so I let my mind wander. A bunch of questions floated through my mind, but when that question about dinosaurs shrinking instead of going extinct drifted by, I NABBED it out of the air and wrote it down. The rest, as they say, is history!

When Danny and Lin's friend Professor Penrod sends them a mysterious package filled with toothy, scratchy Microsaurs hungry enough to chew through walls, they find themselves outnumbered and in over their heads!

MICROSAURS

TINY-RAPTOR PACK ATTACK

DUSTIN HANSEN

**Keep reading for an excerpt.**

It's a good thing we met Professor Penrod when we did, because he needed our help. His trip to China would have been impossible without us to stay behind and keep things in the Microterium running smoothly. And not just that—Lin and I are expert secret keepers, too, which comes in handy, because the Microterium is super top secret.

At first when I saw Professor Penrod's house, it totally gave me the creeps. I actually thought it was a haunted mansion. His house is tucked away in the woods, surrounded by a tall iron gate and overgrown weeds, and snarling dinosaur gargoyles stare down at you from the corners of his roof to finish off the mood. But it didn't worry me anymore. We'd been back every day since we first discovered the Microterium, and now when I saw the house I got all excited, because I knew there were adventures behind that iron gate.

Lin and I slipped between the bars and walked through the weeds behind the spooky old house, toward a rickety old barn.

The Microterium was hidden behind a fake wall inside the barn. Professor Penrod had built the space to keep the Microsaurs he'd rescued safe, happy, and healthy. Oh, and to keep them super top secret. There were more than one hundred of the little dinosaurs living and playing inside the secret jungle hideout, and there was easily room for a thousand more. It really was a Microsaur paradise.

We made our way to the old barn and let ourselves in. The door to the Microterium creaked on its rusty hinges. It took a couple of seconds for my eyes to adjust to the dark as we stepped inside. I looked around for a while, then spotted Professor Penrod's package, right there in the middle of the floor. It was no bigger than one of Lin's little sister's bunny slippers. It was covered in bright red stamps and all kinds of writing and marks that I couldn't read.

"There it is," I said to Lin, and we knelt down for a closer look.

"It's not very big. I was hoping for something huge! Something really growly and awesome," Lin said.

"Those are airholes punched in the top," I said.

"Yeah, and check out the label," Lin said.

A bright yellow sticker was stretched across the top of the box. On it were printed a few, not-so-comforting words:

**⚠ CAUTION**

**Contents may bite.**

**HARD**

"Oh man. I wonder what's inside," I said. I leaned closer. I could hear a tiny scratching, clicking noise that totally gave me the willies. The noise was coming from a spot in the front of the package, where the little creatures had almost chomped through. "They're trying to bite their way out."

Lin jumped up and sprang to the back wall. Professor Penrod was pretty careful about keeping the Microterium secret. The room we were in was a cross between a barn and a science lab, but if you twisted a framed picture of his favorite childhood dog, Bruno, who was dressed as a clown in the photo, the back wall would lower, opening up to the massive Microterium. Lin gave the photo a twist.

"I can't believe he sent us a box full of toothy, scratchy Microsaurs. That is so AWESOME!" she said as the wall started to move.

"Yeah, if you love microsized prehistoric beasts with teeth that chew through walls, then it is really awesome," I said and even while I said it I could feel electric shivers buzzing up my spine.

"I know, RIGHT!?" Lin said. "It's exactly what the Microterium needs. CHOMPERS!"

"Actually, I'm more of a 'eats grass and stomps in mud puddles' kind of guy," I said.

"Come on, Danny. Let's shrink and get a better look," Lin said. She was standing on a metal step beneath one of Professor Penrod's fantastic inventions, the Shrink-A-Fier. It was built right into the Microterium. Copper tubing wound around to cool the liquid boiling in a glass bulb the shape and size of a pumpkin, and a nozzle that looked like a big shiny showerhead gleamed in the sunshine that came in through the roof of the Microterium.

"Um, I'm thinking I'd rather meet these guys for the first time when I'm eighty times their size," I said.

"No way. NO WAY! Dude. We've got to see them eye to eye. You know what they say: You only have one chance to make a first impression," Lin said. She was bouncing up and down on the metal step, which also happened to be the trigger that started up the Shrink-A-Fier. A motor whirled overhead, and the shrinking liquid started to flow into the copper pipes.

"Yeah, I was just hoping that the first impression I made on these guys was less bite-sized," I said nervously.

I scooped up the package and placed it right next to the Shrink-A-Fier. Then I unloaded

*The Bolt* and the upgrade parts and stacked them neatly next to the package of Microsaurs. I cleared my throat, stood up straight and brave, then I joined Lin on the metal step.

"Why did you do that?" Lin asked.

"The parts are heavy, and besides, I wanted to get a close-up look at *The Bolt*'s engine after we are Shrink-A-Fied. It's running pretty good, but I think I might be able to tweak a bit more power out of it," I said.

Lin snapped her helmet strap under her chin as she prepared for an adventure. "I'm good with more power," she said, then gave me a wink. "I love the Shrink-A-Fier. It always makes me feel like a snowflake. You ready?"

"No. Not really," I said, but it was too late. The shrinking had already begun.